Tom McCaughren

The Children
of the Forge

Illustrated by Terry Myler

THE CHILDREN'S PRESS

To Brendan and Nuala McGlynn,
and their children
Paraic, Fiona, Daragh and Niamh

First published in 1985 by
The Children's Press
an imprint of Anvil Books
45 Palmerston Road, Dublin 6
New edition 1992

4 6 5 3

ISBN 0 947962 69 7

Typesetting by Computertype Limited
Printed by Colour Books Limited

CONTENTS

Map labels: NORTHERN IRELAND, REPUBLIC, DUBLIN, WICKLOW, Woodenbridge, ARKLOW

The Children of the Forge

INTRODUCTION

This story takes place against the backdrop of a gold-rush that occurred near Woodenbridge in County Wicklow and the part played in it by a local schoolmaster.

The gold-rush is recorded in the bulletin of the Geological Survey of Ireland as having begun early in September 1795 when news got around that gold was to be found in the sands and gravels of a river that flows from Croghan Mountain. Not surprisingly the river came to be known as the Gold Mines River.

According to an article in the bulletin by T.J. Reeves, normal work immediately ceased in the area as everybody set about the search. He quoted sources as saying that 'about 300 women at one time, besides great numbers of men and children' were at work, using household tools such as shovels, bowls and sieves. In their efforts to work as much ground as possible, their washings were hurried, with the result that much gold escaped their search, so much in fact that the waste heaps afforded a profit on reworking.

This state of affairs, he wrote, persisted until 15 October 1795 when a party of Kildare militia was despatched from Arklow to take possession of the deposit by order of the Government. The local gold-diggers, he added, retired peaceably.

Official mining began the following year. The principal object was said to be 'to endeavour to collect all the gold deposited and thereby remove every temptation for the assembling of mobs, whose numbers had before that time increased to a very alarming degree.'

Figures given in the article showed that during the six weeks of the gold-rush local people found gold worth between £3,000 and £10,000. That may not seem much money now but it was a lot in those days. The finds included a number of substantial nuggets, one weighing 22 ounces. However, the Government operation only produced gold worth £3,675. It cost almost twice that to extract, and the work was abandoned in 1803. Local people continued to wash for gold and between then and 1840 are estimated to have collected almost £20,000 worth. A 24 ounce nugget was reported to have been found in 1856.

The article recorded that the earliest prospecting in the area appeared to have been undertaken around 1770 'by a local schoolmaster named Dunaghoo'. According to an article by William Dick in *Technology Ireland*, the original discovery 'was made by a schoolteacher in approximately 1775'.

Whatever the actual date of the discovery, it is said that for at least ten years prior to the gold-rush, a Dublin jeweller bought four or five ounces of gold each year from a person in the area. A boy was also reported to have found a nugget of gold while fishing in the same river, but in view of the story told by an old man who had seen the gold-rush, I think it's reasonable to assume that the person who was selling gold in Dublin each year was Donaghoo.

The old man's account of how the schoolmaster's discovery became public knowledge, including his ill-fated romance with a local girl, was related by Dr

Diarmaid Ó Muirithe of University College Dublin in a newspaper article some years ago.

Dr Ó Muirithe wrote that the peasantry who took part in the gold-rush struck it rich and according to reliable reports, 'became so independent in places they had the temerity to go on horseback to the big house to enquire if they could buy their little farms out'.

Significant amounts of gold were also found in other rivers that flow from Croghan Mountain, but the sands of the Gold Mines River were said to be the richest by far. Over the years various private companies have continued to search for gold on the mountain, and at one stage prospecting for the 'mother lode' or original vein was said to be extensive. Even today a mining company is exploring for gold in the general area.

The Money Tree which features in *The Children of the Forge* may be seen at the side of the main Dublin-Limerick Road, between Portlaoise and Mountrath. It's near the site of the sixth-century monastery and school founded by St Fintan. For the purpose of the story I have merely 'transplanted' it in my imagination to County Wicklow. The Healing Tree mentioned is one I came across some years ago when, as a news correspondent, I went on an assignment to Cyprus. It was growing near Kykko Monastery in the Troodos Mountains, and the belief that it has healing powers is closely associated with the history of the monastery.

Tom McCaughren
1992

1 THE PROSPECTOR

It all started the day Stumpy Joe brought the pony into the forge to have it shod. He knew about the gold, but he didn't know about the curse, and no one thought of telling him.

A short time earlier Maggie's voice could be heard calling 'Ginnie, gin, gin, gin,' to let the white goat know they were ready to milk her. Ginnie was munching away at a clump of weeds in a piece of waste ground—you could hardly call it a garden—opposite the door of the forge. When she heard Maggie's voice she lifted her head and looked around, ignored her and continued nibbling at the weeds.

'Ah, there you are,' smiled Maggie, and she hobbled between rusty harrows, old horse-drawn ploughs and other farm implements that had been brought in for mending once upon a time and somehow forgotten. 'Fraggle,' she shouted, 'she's over here.'

A moment later her brother Fergal ran in from the flower garden in front of the cottage attached to the forge. He placed a red plastic bucket under Ginnie's udder, and kneeling down on his long lanky legs, pressed his dark head against her white side. Maggie talked to her and tickled her between the horns to keep her still, and he began squeezing the milk into the bucket.

Their grandfather, who used to be the blacksmith and was now retired, liked a drop of goat's milk. Indeed, he was the only one who did. Everyone else, including the children, thought it was too strong. However, Fergal and Maggie didn't mind doing the job of milking for him. It could be great fun.

Fergal looked up and, with a mischievous glint in his eye, said, 'What do you think, Maggie? Do you think grandad's only joking when he says my wart will go away if I rub it on the goat's udder every time I milk her?'

Maggie leaned over to see if the wart on his knuckle was getting any smaller, only to have a stream of warm milk squirted into her eyes. 'Stop it,' she yelled, and shielding her face with her hand hobbled out of range as fast as the calliper on her right leg could carry her. 'Stop it, or I'll tell grandad on you.'

Fergal smiled and continued squeezing the milk into the bucket. The goat looked up and moved forward. 'Stay still, Ginnie,' he urged. 'Here, that's the girl, stay still now.'

'Serves you right,' said Maggie, wiping her eyes with the back of her hand. She had fuzzy hair falling into ringlets in places, and several drops of milk had lodged in her tiny curls. Lowering her head, she shook it vigorously, saying, 'She can wander all over the garden now for all I care.'

Just then their friend Pernickety arrived.

'Ah, the very man I need,' said Fergal. 'Here Pernickety, give me a hand.'

'What do you want me to do?'

'Hold her still for a minute.'

Pernickety, who lived up the road, didn't particularly trust the goats at the forge. Whatever about the white one, the black billy-goat would sometimes lower his head and butt any one who wasn't nimble enough to hop out of his way.

'Come on,' urged Fergal, 'she won't bite you.'

Pernickety, who was very precise about everything, adjusted his glasses and ventured closer.

'Don't trust him,' warned Maggie, but it was too late. With a triumphant cry of delight, Fergal aimed one of Ginnie's teats upwards again and sprayed Pernickety's glasses with milk.

Pernickety jumped back, stumbling blindly into a concrete roller that was used for rolling fields, and tumbled head over heels into the weeds. Ginnie decided she had had enough and hopped up on to a pile of old stones in the corner where she stood chewing her cud.

Maggie decided she had had enough of Fergal's carry-on too, and as Pernickety picked himself up and removed his glasses, she brushed some milk from her skirt and began looking around for a stick.

Seeing that she was getting mad at him, Fergal mocked her and high-stepped across the machinery with his bucket of milk. He had just reached the flower garden when a voice with a very pronounced Northern accent said, 'Hallo there ! Anybody home?'

They all stopped what they were doing and looked out to see a small stocky man with a brown pony standing at the gate. He was very short, almost dwarfish, with broad shoulders and a big head more befitting a tall man, and resting almost on his bushy black eyebrows was a tattered cowboy hat.

'Well?' he said.

'Well what?' asked Fergal.

'Is there anybody in?'

'Who do you mean?' asked Maggie.

'The smith, of course. Is he in at all?'

'Well, I dunno,' said Maggie.

'Can't you find out?' said the stranger. 'Tell him there's a man at the gate called Stumpy Joe.'

While Maggie and Fergal rushed into the house to tell their grandfather someone was looking for him, Pernickety wiped the milk from his glasses, placed them very precisely on the bridge of his nose and hooked them behind his ears. In spite of the fact that he was younger than the others, his glasses, resting beneath his fringe of fair, almost white, hair gave him a rather studious look.

'Well, Scholar,' said the stranger in a very cocky fashion, 'what are you lookin' at then?'

'Nothing,' mumbled Pernickety. 'It's just that...'

'Just what? Have I got two heads or somethin'?'

Pernickety shook his head, took to his heels and ran in after the others.

Opening the gate, the stranger led the pony through the large stone doorway shaped like a horseshoe. A few minutes later the children arrived in the forge with their grandfather, and the little man held out his hand saying, 'I'm Stumpy Joe. Pleased to meet you.'

'What can I do for you?' asked their grandfather.

'Shoe the pony, of course,' and before the old man could explain that he no longer worked as a blacksmith, Stumpy Joe had unstrapped a pack that included pots and pans and a short-handled shovel from the pony's back and dumped it in a corner.

The children watched their grandfather, who was still stout and strong for his age, run an experienced hand down along the pony's sagging back. 'Sure she's only a bag of bones,' he said.

'Maybe you'd rather sell me one of the ponies out there in the field then?'

Maggie was about to protest, but there was no need. Her grandfather told him, 'They're the children's.'

Stumpy Joe gave his own pony a firm pat on the neck and said, 'Ah, appearances can be deceivin'. There's plenty of life in this girl yet. And sure if I had no use for her there'd be nowhere for her but the glue factory.'

The old man sighed. 'I suppose you're right. Nobody has time for horses any more. It's all go now, dashing here and dashing there.'

Even as they spoke the roar of a low-flying aircraft filled the forge. Frightened by the noise, half a dozen hens rushed in from the back yard and skidded past them.

'And there's no such thing as peace and quiet any more,' observed Stumpy Joe. 'Your man's flying a bit low, isn't he?'

The old man looked up and nodded. 'It's the Sheik.'

'It's a private plane,' Fergal explained. 'It belongs to the Arabs.'

'Arabs?' repeated Stumpy Joe. 'And what would Arabs be doin' down here in the middle of Wicklow?'

'They've bought the Manor,' Maggie informed him. 'They fly in and out from the Middle East.'

'From Lebanon,' added Pernickety.

'Wherever they're from, they must be rollin' in the oul' spondulicks.' Stumpy Joe sounded envious.

'The what?' asked Pernickety.

'Spondulicks—money. You'd wonder what would bring the likes of them here.'

'More to the point,' said the old man. 'What brings you here?'

'Me? Sure amn't I goin' to be rich myself some day. It's only a matter of findin' it, that's all.'

'Finding what?' asked Maggie.

'Gold!' said Stumpy Joe as if she should have known what he was talking about. 'Isn't there gold here in the Wicklow hills?'

'Maybe,' said the old man. 'And maybe not.'

'From what I hear,' said Stumpy Joe, 'it's just lying around waitin' for some enterprisin' fella like myself to come along and find it.'

The old man smiled and the children tittered.

'Oh you can laugh if you like,' said Stumpy Joe, 'but if it's been found once, it can be found again.'

'Sure nobody's ever found anything worth talking about,' said Fergal.

'That's not the way I heard it,' said Stumpy Joe. 'One man found enough to make himself rich.'

'You mean the school-teacher?' asked Pernickety.

'Now you have it, Scholar, now you have it. If he could do it, why can't I do it? Now, about the pony. I wouldn't walk the hills myself without shoes, and I wouldn't ask the pony to do it either.'

Maggie looked at her grandfather, and it was her imploring look more than anything Stumpy Joe had said that made him purse his lips and nod his head in agreement. 'All right,' he said, 'but I'm only doing it for the pony's sake. By right you should be turning her out to graze.'

'And what else will she be doin'?' asked Stumpy Joe. 'Sure when she's walkin' through the hills with me she'll have all the time in the world to graze.'

'And what about all that gold you're going to find?' asked Fergal. 'Who's going to carry that for you?'

Stumpy Joe winked at him. 'Sure when I find that I'll come back here and ask you young ones to come and give me a hand.'

They all laughed, and whatever misgivings the old man might have had about the pony he had decided she would be better off with shoes than without them. So he took down the leather apron that he hadn't worn for years and put it on.

'Now Fergal,' he said, 'reach me some of these old newspapers to see if I can get this fire going.'

He stuffed a handful of newspapers and some plastic bags into the furnace, put a match to them and switched on the electric bellows.

For some reason or other the old man seemed to take a liking to Stumpy Joe. Perhaps it was because of his cheerful manner, or the way he talked. More likely it was because he seemed to care enough about the pony to want her shod. Whatever the reason, it wasn't long before they were talking about horses. As they did so, the old man lifted several pieces of fancy wrought-iron work that his son had been making and laid them against some modern welding equipment. Then, with loving care, he took out his hammers and tongs and laid them on the anvil. Seeing that the fire was coming on nicely, but wasn't yet hot enough, he got a long metal pole and reaching up to a dusty beam took down one old shoe after another. He gave each of them a good bang against the anvil to knock the dust off and explained that they were surgical shoes.

'That's a rocker shoe,' he said, and the children crowded closer. 'I made that for a horse with a diseased hoof. It gave it relief by keeping the blood circulating. And that one, with the gap in it, that was for a horse with a corn. The gap eased the pressure on it. And this is a brushing shoe. I made it for a horse that had one hoof brushing against the other. See how it's shaped to make it throw the hoof out and away from the other one. . .'

So it went on, and while the old man reminisced about days gone by he began making shoes for Stumpy Joe's pony. Putting pieces of iron into the fire, he brought them out with the tongs when they were red-hot and placing them on the anvil, tapped and turned them until the sparks were flying and the hammer was dancing and singing as if it had a mind of its own. Soon he was cradling the pony's hooves in his lap, cleaning and paring them with a skill of a lifetime, and it wasn't long before the forge was filled with the pungent smell of burning hoof, as the shoes were measured and fitted. Finally, the nail ends were twisted off and filed close to the hoof.

The old man straightened up and wiped away the beads of sweat that had gathered on his few remaining strands of hair. 'There you are. That should do.'

'A work of art,' observed Stumpy Joe approvingly. 'Now, what do I owe you?'

'No charge,' replied the old man, 'so long as you look after the pony.' He took off his apron, and hanging it back in its place, added as a sort of afterthought, 'If you've a few pence to spare you could do worse than put it in the Money Tree. That's what people usually do when they're looking for something, and you'll need all the help you can get if you're to find your gold.'

'You mean I could make a wish?' asked Stumpy Joe. When the old man nodded he inquired, 'And where would I find this Money Tree?'

'At the old monastery. The children will show you.'

As the old man put away his tools, Stumpy Joe went outside and sat down beside the children on a flat circular stone. It was a stone with a hole in the middle which had been used in times past to hold a wheel while the rim was put on. 'What's all this about a Money Tree?' he asked, lighting a cigarette.

'People hammer coins into it and make a wish,' Fergal explained.

'And does the wish come true?'

'Sometimes,' said Maggie, looking down at the calliper on her leg. 'Not always.'

Pernickety, who was still trying to make out just what sort of person Stumpy Joe was, asked him, 'Why do you wear a cowboy hat?'

'Because I'm a prospector,' he said. 'That's why.' He flicked the ash of his cigarette into the hole in the stone, and took off the hat so that they could have a closer look at it. It was flat-topped, curly-brimmed, and stained from the sweat of many years' wear.

They were all wondering if the real reason he wore it was because he had such a big head when he explained, 'This hat used to belong to my grandfather. He got it when he was prospectin' for gold in the Klondike.'

'Where's that?' asked Fergal.

'In North America. He was there during the great gold rush at the end of the last century, and he brought it back with him.'

'Did he bring any gold back?' asked Pernickety.

'Of course he did. Sure he found nuggets as big as your fist and came home a rich man.'

'What did he do with all his money?' asked Fergal.

'Well, it was like this.' Stumpy Joe put the hat back on his head. 'In all them days up in the Klondike, in all that snow and frost, away beyond civilization, never a drink passed his lips. For ten years he scraped and dug at the frozen ground, and when he had made his fortune he decided he was going to come back home, buy his own distillery and drink whiskey until it was comin' out of his ears.'

Fergal laughed. 'You're codding.'

'I am not,' he said. 'As God's my judge. I suppose he also wanted to make it up to my grandmother for being away so long, especially with her havin' a wooden leg and all.'

The others were smiling now too, and seeing they were beginning to warm to him he went on, 'It's true. She had a wooden leg. How else do you think I got the name Stumpy Joe?'

They all broke out laughing, and he added, 'Then a dreadful thing happened.'

'What?' asked Pernickety.

'My grandfather got a terrible fit of remorse and went all religious. He decided to mend his ways, so he ups and sells the distillery. But what was worse, he opened up every tap in the place and poured all the whiskey out into the river. Well, you should have seen the local people. Sure I believe they nearly drank the river dry. My grandmother had to take to the bed and couldn't get up for three days.'

'She must have been very upset,' said Maggie.

'Upset?' said Stumpy Joe. 'Divil the bit. She was so drunk she couldn't put on her wooden leg.'

They all burst out laughing and Fergal asked him, 'Where else have you been? I mean, besides the North and here. You are from the North, aren't you?'

Stumpy Joe nodded. 'I am surely. But I'm a man of the world. Anywhere there's a horse fair, I've been at it. I even worked as a cheapjack over in the West when I wasn't at the fair in Ballinasloe'.

'What's a cheapjack?' asked Maggie.

'It's what the people over there call somebody who sells second-hand clothes. I had a van and whenever things were slack in the horse business, I'd go along to a town and set up shop.'

'What sort of thing did you say to people to get them to buy second-hand clothes?' asked Pernickety.

The little man smiled. 'You should know by now, Scholar, I was never a one to be short of a few words.' So saying, he hopped up on the stone, pretended he was selling clothes, and recited with the rapidity of a machine gun:

> *Double depth and tipped on both ends,*
> *Guaranteed neither to burn, crack or wear out,*

*To wash like a child's bottom, and pull like an ass in
    holt,
Catch fleas lying, flying, standing up, asleep or
    awake,
To have 99 out of a hundred,
The rest go to Fiddlers Green where the fleas stop in
    winter.*

They all laughed heartily again, and Maggie shook
her head saying, 'Joe, you're the limit.'

'What does it mean, "an ass in holt"?' Pernickety
asked him.

'I don't know. Maybe it means bogged down.'

'And what's Fiddlers Green?' asked Fergal.

'Ah, that's nine miles below hell, where the fleas
stop for winter.'

When they had stopped laughing, Stumpy Joe sat
down and reflected, 'Aye, them were the days. But
there's no money in horses any more. That's why I'm
prospectin'. If my grandfather could find gold, then
maybe so can I.'

'Granny had a gold nugget once,' Maggie told him.
'She found it when she was a child. But I don't know
where it is now. She's dead.'

'There you are,' he said, slapping his leg, 'what did I
tell you? There's gold here in Wicklow too, if you
know where to look for it.'

'But sure if people knew where to look for it, it
would have been found long ago,' said Fergal.

'True, but you know what they say. In the land of
the blind the one-eyed man is king.'

'What do you mean?' asked Pernickety.

'Well, you see, it's not just a question of knowing

where to look. You have to know what to look for, and I know, for my grandfather told me.'

Fergal and Maggie's father came through the forge from the back yard where he had been making a sheep-pen for a local farmer, and told them their lunch was ready. Their mother appeared too, probably out of curiosity to see who had got the old man to open the forge, and said to Stumpy Joe, 'Maybe you could eat a boiled egg?'

The little man got up, and taking off his cowboy hat with a sweep that would have done justice to Buffalo Bill, told her, 'Well you know, Missus, I once met a man who ate two of them and he's still alive.'

They all laughed at his funny sense of humour, and took him up the back yard to the new bungalow for something to eat. Afterwards, Fergal and Maggie showed him their ponies, Silver and Star. The ponies had trotted over to the back gate, and Joe climbed up

the bars to look them over. Having examined their teeth like the expert he was, he fondled the ears of the brown one with the white patch on its forehead, and said, 'The grey one's nice, but this is the one I'd go for.'

Maggie smiled. 'That's Star. She's mine.'

A short time later, Stumpy Joe strapped the prospecting pack on to the back of his own pony and waddled up the road towards the hills.

'Do you think he'll find anything?' asked Fergal.

'Who knows?' said his grandfather. 'Did you show him the Money Tree?'

Fergal shook his head. 'He was more interested in the ponies. '

'But he's making a wish,' said Maggie. 'He gave us ten pence to put into the tree for him.'

'Well, I hope it brings him luck,' said the old man. 'If he finds what he's looking for, he's going to need it.'

The children looked at him, puzzled, and Pernickety asked, 'If he finds the gold, what more could he wish for?'

'Ah, you're forgetting, Pernickety,' said the old man, 'you're forgetting what happened the schoolmaster.'

'You mean there's some sort of curse on the gold?'

'Mmmm, I suppose you might say that. It didn't do him much good anyway. . . '

2 UNEXPECTED VISITORS

Shortly after Stumpy Joe had headed for the hills to do some prospecting with his newly shod pony, a long black limousine slid silently to a halt outside the forge.

Fergal and Maggie were at the back watching their father putting the finishing touches to the sheep-pen, when their mother ran down the yard calling to them, 'It's the Sheik. It's the Sheik!'

Their father switched off the welding torch and took off his protective mask. 'The what?' he asked.

'It's the Sheik. He's stopped out on the road.'

'What does he want?'

His wife shook her head saying, 'I don't know.'

Before they could discuss the matter further a man in a dark blue uniform and matching peaked cap came through into the yard. It was the chauffeur. The children watched, wondering what was going on.

'Hi ya, Paddy,' said their father, and the two men

shook hands. 'What brings you here?'

Paddy Mac, as he was known, used to have a car-hire firm in the town, but had given it up to work full time for the people who had bought the Manor. 'Mr. Baracat would like to visit the Money Tree.'

'Sure he doesn't have to have our permission for that.'

'I know,' said Paddy Mac, 'but he asked me to ask you anyway. I suppose he knows the way some of the locals resent him coming in and buying up the Manor.'

'It's a free country. The path to the Money Tree may go over our fields, but it's a public right-of-way. Anyone can use it.'

'It's all right then?'

'Of course. Fergal and Maggie will go with you if you like.'

'Much obliged. I think Mr. Baracat would like that.'

Fergal and Maggie could see that several people had appeared now out of sheer curiosity, for while they had occasionally seen the big black limousine gliding along the country roads between the Manor and the town, they had never actually seen the man they called the Sheik. Their grandfather was standing at the forge, and Pernickety, who had gone home for lunch, had come out with his parents to the gate of their house farther up the road. Of all the people who had visited the monastery and the Money Tree over the years, none had ever created such interest.

Having nicknamed the foreigner who had bought the Manor, the Sheik, the local people no doubt had formed a certain image in their minds. However, the man who came through from the road was not wearing Arab dress, nor were those with him. He was immaculately dressed in a blue pin-stripe suit, with a maroon tie and matching handkerchief which protruded ever so slightly from his breast pocket. He had black hair, turning grey, that swept back from a sharply pointed hairline, and a dark moustache, all of which gave his swarthy Middle Eastern features what the women in the area were later to call a handsome look not unlike that of the actor Omar Sharif. In one hand he carried a short, silver-handled cane, and in the other he held the hand of a black-haired, sallow-faced boy.

The boy was casually dressed in a cream-coloured jacket and light blue trousers. He walked awkwardly with the aid of a stick, and keeping a motherly eye on him was an attractive young woman. She was following at what seemed to be a discreet distance, something the onlookers assumed was in keeping with Arab tradition. Yet her dress was far from traditional. She wore a smart blue two-piece suit, with her hair tucked up under a matching pillbox hat, and she looked more European than the others.

Fussing around the Sheik and the boy was a short, stout man with a bald head and a moustache. He wore a dark jacket with gold bands on the ends of his sleeves, and he repeatedly wiped the sweat from his brow with a handkerchief as if the exertion of continually trying to please them was almost too much for him. Having inquired from Paddy what the position was, he confided the information to his master.

Mr. Baracat looked around and smiled at those standing in the yard. 'Thank you,' he said in perfect English, before following Fergal and Maggie into the back field.

By this time Pernickety, anxious not to miss anything, had come in from the road and crossed the field to join them. 'What's up?' he panted.

'They want to see the Money Tree,' Fergal told him.

Pernickety trotted to keep up, and casting a glance back at the Sheik and his entourage, remarked, 'That's funny. Why should they want to see the Money Tree?'

'Maybe they want to make a wish,' said Maggie.

'What could they wish for?' asked Fergal. 'With their money they must have everything they want.'

'Anyway,' said Maggie, 'it's none of your business. If they want to see our Money Tree they've as much right as anybody else.'

Maggie hobbled on. In spite of her handicap she could move fairly fast, and the other two quickened their pace to keep up with her. They were all anxious that the people from the Manor shouldn't get too close to them, for while they didn't mind showing them the way to the Money Tree, they didn't want to be seen to be too friendly with them.

The reason for this went back to the time the estate had been put up for sale. Confident that no one would be able to pay the millions of pounds needed to buy it, local farmers had planned to purchase sections of the land to add to their own. As a result, they had been deeply disappointed when a rich oil sheik had come in and paid an astronomical price for the lot. Some of the farmers had just harboured resentment and decided to have nothing to do with the foreigners. Others had persuaded themselves that the low-flying aircraft was causing their cows to give less milk and their hens to lay fewer eggs, and entertained thoughts of legal action for damages. A few, inevitably, had been tempted to take a different kind of action, and there had been one or two unpleasant incidents. Someone had let dogs loose among the Sheik's sheep, driving a number of them to destruction, while threatening and abusive slogans had been painted on the walls at the main entrance. Most people, of course, didn't agree with that sort of thing, yet even the children knew it wouldn't do to be seen to be too friendly with their new neighbours.

The Money Tree was a very old and rather scraggy sycamore that grew at a secluded corner of the monastery. Over the years, as it had come to be revered more and more, a wall had been built around it to mark it out from other trees and indicate that it occupied a special place, not only in the history of the monastery, but in the community.

The Sheik's group followed Paddy Mac through the small gateway, while Fergal, Maggie and Pernickety stood aside and watched them over the wall. For a moment the visitors stood silently looking at the tree and the thousands of coins, many twisted and bent, that had been hammered into its ancient trunk. Then the Sheik took a coin from his pocket and handed it to the small fat man, who in turn handed it to Paddy Mac. Paddy Mac took the coin in his gloved hand, walked over to the tree, and with a fancy little hammer proceeded to drive it into the trunk. When this was done, he stepped back and leaned against the wall to talk to the children.

'What are they doing?' whispered Pernickety, who was standing on his toes to see over the wall.

'Making a wish,' said Paddy Mac. 'What do you think? '

The Sheik and his son were now standing at the foot

of the Money Tree, their heads bowed, eyes closed, saying a silent prayer.

'I wonder what they're wishing for?' said Maggie, more to herself than anybody else.

Paddy Mac leaned closer and confided, 'They've got their own problems.'

The short stout man dabbed his sweating brow with his handkerchief once more, and waited for the Sheik and his son to finish.

'Who's he?' asked Fergal.

Paddy Mac pointed to his own sleeve as much as to say, did they not see the gold bands on the man's sleeves, and whispered behind his upraised hand, 'That's Ahmed, the pilot.'

The Sheik and his son were turning to go now. Ahmed opened the gate and ushered them out and Paddy Mac followed. The children cut across to the path ahead of them, and led the way back down to the forge.

On the way through the yard, the Sheik turned to Maggie and Fergal's mother who was standing at the bungalow door, and with a slight bow of his head said, 'Thank you.' He had a similar word of thanks for their grandfather out on the road, before helping his son up into the back seat of their car and climbing in himself.

Before they drove off, the Sheik leaned forward and said something to Ahmed, who in turn had a word with Paddy Mac. Getting back out of the car, Paddy Mac walked over to the children and taking out a fistful of coins handed each of them £1, saying, 'Mr. Baracat asked me to give you something for taking him up to the Money Tree.' They all protested, and their grandfather said it wasn't necessary, but Paddy Mac

insisted, explaining that Mr. Baracat would be offended if they didn't take it.

During the entire visit, the boy had said nothing.
Now as they drove off, he leaned forward, smiled out
at them and gave a little wave. Instinctively they waved
back.

When Fergal came in from the yard next morning, he
heard his mother declaring, 'I don't care what anyone
says, I think he's very nice.'

'Who's very nice?' he asked.

His father, who was just finishing his breakfast, cast
his eyes up to heaven, and told him, 'Who do you
think? The Sheik of course.'

Fergal put down a bowl full of eggs which he had
just collected from the hen-house, and said to his
mother, 'But you were complaining about him only
last week.'

'That's right,' said his father, 'you said that aero-
plane of his was putting the hens off laying.'

'Well I've changed my mind. I think he's very nice.'

'So do I,' said Maggie, buttering another slice of
toast. 'As a matter of fact, I think he's gorgeous.'

'Ah, talking about me again,' smiled her grandfather
who had heard her last remark as he opened the door.
'Fergal, pour me a drop of tea there like a good lad.'

'If there's any left,' said Fergal.

'Here,' said his mother, 'I'll make a fresh drop.'

'What do you think, grandad?' continued Maggie.
'Isn't he gorgeous?'

'You mean the Sheik?'

'Who else? Isn't he the spitting image of Omar
Sharif?'

'Omar who?'

'Oh grandad! You know well who I mean. Omar Sharif, the actor.'

'Sure what would I know about these actor fellas. Now, if it was a horse you were talking about. . . 'The old man chuckled to himself and pulled up a chair. 'Here, pass me over the marmalade like a good girl.'

'That's all you men think about,' said Maggie. 'Food ! You've no romance in you at all.'

'That's right,' said her mother. 'All Irishmen are the same. But they'd better watch out with all these handsome strangers coming around.'

'What,' smiled her husband, 'you mean Stumpy Joe?'

Fergal gave a guffaw that sent a shower of crumbs on to the table in front of him.

'Would you look at him,' said his mother in disgust. She gave him a clip on the back of the head and added, 'God help the woman who gets you, smart alec. Just for that you can help to wash up.'

The old man pushed away his cup and saucer and leaned back. 'Isn't it strange,' he reflected, 'how they both called on the same day. One man wishing for riches, and a rich man wishing for something else.'

It was little philosophical gems like this that always made the rest of the family sit up and listen when the old man was talking.

Pernickety came in just as Maggie was saying, 'Do you think Stumpy Joe has any hope of finding gold?'

Her grandfather shrugged, and Pernickety took off his glasses to clean them as they had got steamed up.

'He seems to know what he's talking about,' said Fergal. 'He says his grandfather prospected for gold in the Klondike. Do you think he was having us on?'

'It could well be true,' said the old man. 'Many an Irishman went to America in the last century when they couldn't get a living here, and a lot of them made their way up the Yukon to the Klondike looking for gold. Some of them found it too, but it was hard earned.'

'Do you think Stumpy Joe might strike it rich here in Wicklow?' asked Pernickety. 'You know, like the school-teacher.'

'I never heard that story about the school-teacher,' said Fergal.

'Nor I,' said Maggie. 'Did he really strike it rich?'

The old man smiled. 'Oh, he became rich all right.'

'You mean like the Sheik?' said Maggie.

'Not quite. You see, there was what your mother and yourself would call a bit of romance involved, and that put a stop to his gallop.'

'Will you tell us about it?' said Fergal. 'You said there was some sort of curse on the gold, didn't you?'

'This is no time for story-telling,' said his mother. 'Come on, there's work to be done, both of you. Pernickety seems to know all about it. He can tell you— after you've done the dishes.'

As the two men went out to the yard and their mother went off to make the beds, Fergal and Maggie set about earning their pocket-money by doing the washing-up.

'Do you really know the story about the school-teacher?' Maggie asked Pernickety.

Pernickety, whose glasses had got steamed up again from the hot water, rubbed his eyes and shook his head. 'All I know is that he was the master over there at Woodenbridge. He found gold all right, but whatever happened he had no luck with it.'

'Did you ever wonder,' said Fergal, 'how people like that could be so rich?'

'You mean the Arabs?' asked Pernickety. 'They probably own oil wells in the desert.'

'Then why should they come here?' wondered Fergal.

'You don't think they're after the gold too?' asked Maggie.

Fergal shrugged. 'Why not? There was gold-mining done on the estate at one time, wasn't there?'

Maggie dried her hands. 'You know, you could be right. I'm sure they didn't come here for the good of their health. And you know something else? If that's what they're after, they won't want Stumpy Joe traipsing all over their land looking for it.'

'And I'm sure he has no licence to look for it,' said Pernickety.

'Well, we'll just have to keep an eye out for him and warn him to be careful,' said Fergal. 'If the Arabs are after the gold, they would have the prospecting rights and everything like that all tied up, and I don't think they'd take kindly to someone like Stumpy Joe trying to jump their claim.'

It was several weeks before they saw the little man with the cowboy hat again, and for some reason or other he didn't want to see them.

The town was crowded, as it always was on a Saturday, and their father was edging the car along the main street looking for a parking place, when Maggie spotted a group of men admiring a sprightly little pony at the entrance to the square.

'Look,' she cried, 'it's Stumpy Joe. Blow the horn, dad, blow the horn, quickly.'

Her father obliged and she waved frantically out of the window. The group of men stopped talking and looked over, but Stumpy Joe quickly looked away and pulled the others back into conversation again.

Disappointed, Maggie sat back, saying, 'He didn't see us.'

'I think he did,' said Fergal.

'But he didn't recognize us.'

'I think he did,' said Fergal. 'He just didn't want to know us.'

'Why should he not want to know you?' asked their father. 'That's silly. Maybe he was just in the middle of buying a new pony.'

'It looked to me more like he was selling it,' said Maggie. 'And it seems a nice one too.'

Her father pulled in and switched off the engine. 'Well, let's go back and see what he has to offer. It couldn't be any worse than the one he brought to the forge.'

'It looks a lot livelier anyway,' said Fergal.

Convinced that Stumpy Joe wouldn't deliberately avoid them, Maggie hobbled on ahead. When the others caught up with her, they found her looking around puzzled, for there was no sign of the men, the pony, or Stumpy Joe.

3   AN EXPENSIVE WISH

There was a hole in the trunk of the Money Tree which appeared to be as ancient as the tree itself. It had been formed when a branch had withered and died, and according to tradition it always contained some water, no matter how dry the weather might be. The reason for this strange phenomenon was said to be that when the well of the saint who had founded the monastery was diverted to an adjoining field, the water had remained in the tree. Thus, the water in the tree was looked upon as a sort of holy well. Some of those who came to the Money Tree would dip a finger in the water and bless themselves; others would simply touch the water and say a silent prayer.

Some people also believed that the water in the Money Tree had healing qualities, and Fergal was one of them. He had wet the wart on his knuckle with it many times, and now as he sat with Maggie and

Pernickety in the sunshine, their backs to the stone wall surrounding the tree, he wondered if it was doing any good.

'Maybe you're not doing it right,' suggested Pernickety.

'What can I do, except dip it into it?'

Pernickety adjusted his glasses so that they sat more comfortably on his nose. 'Maybe you should do it the way Tom Sawyer or Huckleberry Finn would do it?'

'And what way's that?'

'Well, these things usually have to be done with some kind of a ritual. You know, like dipping it in at the stroke of midnight, by the light of the moon.'

The others tittered, and Pernickety went on, 'You can laugh if you like, but in olden days things like that were very important. Do you know that they built the great burial mound up at Newgrange in County Meath in such a way that the sun would only shine into it during the winter solstice?'

'What's the winter solstice?' asked Fergal.

'December 21st,' Maggie told him. 'It's the shortest day of the year.'

Fergal was continuing to examine his wart closely. 'You mean it won't work now in the summer?'

'I'm not saying that,' said Pernickety. 'All I'm saying is that in olden days when people built mounds and things, the sun and moon were very important to them. Maybe it was the same with monasteries. Who knows?'

'You mean I should try it by the light of the moon?'

'Well you've tried everything else,' Maggie remarked, 'Rubbing it on the goat's udder hasn't done it any good. Or dipping it in the water at the forge.'

'I never thought it would.'

'And rubbing it with a frog hasn't helped either,' she continued, 'so what have you got to lose?' She paused for a moment before adding, 'I'll come with you if you like, if that's what's worrying you.'

'You mean scared?' said Fergal. 'You must be joking.'

'All right then,' said Pernickety. 'But you'll have to do it right. It'll have to be on the stroke of midnight.'

Fergal nodded. 'Okay, you can show me how.'

'Who me?' Pernickety got up to go. 'What can I do?'

'You're the one who suggested it,' smiled Maggie, 'so you'll have to come along to make sure he does it right.'

'I don't know if I can get out.'

'You wouldn't be scared, now would you?' teased Maggie.

Pernickety took off his glasses and rubbed his eyes. 'What's there to be scared of?'

'Oh, I don't know,' continued Maggie. 'Maybe you're afraid some monks might jump up and catch you. They say the monastery is haunted, you know.'

Pernickety put his glasses back on and composed himself. 'It so happens I don't believe in things like that. Anyway, I never heard it was haunted.'

'Look, are you going to come or not?' asked Fergal.

'Can't you say you're staying late at our house,' said Maggie. 'Then we can come up here when we're leaving you home.'

'Good idea,' said Fergal. 'Come on, I'm going back down home.'

The moon was high in the sky as three shadowy figures

made their way along the path towards the ruins of the monastery. Normally those who trod this path walked in single file, but that was in the daytime; now it was night. The boys had suggested that Maggie should take the path and they would walk beside her in case she might trip and fall. Somehow she suspected that their gallantry was not unconnected with a desire to stay closer together. Nevertheless, as she pulled her collar up around her and looked at the dark outline of the monastery ruins, she was glad to have them by her side.

'How will we know it's midnight?' whispered Fergal. 'I can't even see my watch, let alone the time.'

'My digital,' said Maggie. 'I've set the alarm for 12.'

They hurried on. Lights twinkled in the houses along the road and down towards the town. Now and then a dog barked, but otherwise the countryside was dark and quiet, so quiet that the gravel at the gateway to the Money Tree sounded very noisy as it crunched under their feet.

Fergal opened the gate and led the way in. 'I hope the moon's still out when the time comes.'

The others looked up to see the moon grinning down between several patches of dark cloud, and followed him over to the Money Tree.

'Put your hand into it,' Pernickety told him. 'It must be nearly time.'

'What's that?' said Maggie.

'What?' asked Fergal.

'I thought I heard something in the corner.'

'Probably a rat,' remarked Pernickety.

'Oh come on,' said Maggie, speaking to herself and to her digital watch. 'Come on, bleep.'

Almost as if the watch had heard her, the bleeps of

midnight came to their ears. At the same time, the moon went in behind the clouds, darkness descended on the Money Tree, and there was another movement in the corner as if someone was scrambling up on to the wall. They jumped back, the bleeps stopped and the moon came out again.

'Look,' cried Maggie in horror. 'It's a monk!'

Looking up, the others were just in time to see the outline of a hooded figure hurrying along the top of the wall and disappearing into the deep shadows of the monastery.

It was impossible to say who got out through the gate first; even Maggie was surprised at how quickly she moved as they raced for home, all thought of warts forgotten.

Taking refuge in the welding shop, they closed the door behind them and switched on the light. They were trembling and out of breath, and it was a few minutes before any of them could speak.

'I thought you were only joking when you said the monastery was haunted,' panted Pernickety.

'So I was,' Maggie told him.

'What do you think it was then?' asked Fergal. 'It looked like a monk.'

'That's right,' Pernickety recalled. 'He was fat too, just like Friar Tuck.' He stopped talking to catch his breath again, then asked Fergal, 'What's that you have in your hand?'

Fergal was fidgeting with a piece of paper, rolling and unrolling it absent-mindedly as he thought of what they had seen. 'Just a piece of paper,' he said. 'I must have picked it up when I put my hand into the water.'

'That's not just a piece of paper,' exclaimed Pernickety. 'That's a bank-note!'

Fergal unrolled the paper and the other two came closer to see. 'So it is,' he gasped. 'It's a . . . a . . .'

'A £50 note,' whispered Maggie.

'An English £50 note,' said Pernickety. 'Look, it's got the Queen on it.'

'I must have closed my hand on it with the fright,' said Fergal.

'But who would have put it there?' wondered Pernickety, wide-eyed at the sight of so much money.

'It can't have been there long,' said Fergal, examining it. 'It's hardly even wet.'

'The monk,' said Maggie. 'He must have left it. But what am I saying, he couldn't have been a monk. They're all dead.'

'Maybe they're trying to tell us something,' suggested Fergal.

'The monastery hasn't been used for hundreds of

years,' Maggie argued. 'They're all gone now. There's not even a sign of their graves.'

'And the money is modern,' Pernickety pointed out. 'Look, it's brand new.'

As they examined the note more closely, Pernickety continued, 'Somebody must want something very badly to leave as much as that at the Money Tree.'

'Whoever it was should know they can't buy their wish,' said Maggie. 'The coins that are put in are only a token, you know, a sort of tradition.'

'Anyway,' said Fergal, 'nobody would have money like that to throw away, unless they'd struck it rich.'

'You mean someone like Stumpy Joe?' asked Maggie. 'Or the Arabs?'

'That's it,' said Fergal. 'It could be the Arabs.'

'That's the way some of them dress too,' added Pernickety. 'You know, with things over their head.'

'Ahmed, the pilot,' said Fergal. 'He's built like Friar Tuck. Do you think it might have been him?'

Maggie nodded. 'You might have something there. And he did seem to be worrying a lot when we saw him. I wonder if he's up to something?'

'What?' asked Pernickey. 'Like using his plane for smuggling or something?'

'Could be, 'said Fergal. 'Maybe he's even found the gold and is flying it out of the country.'

'And is afraid he'll be caught,' said Maggie. 'So after visiting the Money Tree with the Sheik, he decides to make a wish for himself . . . a wish that he won't be found out.'

'Not being a Christian,' said Fergal, 'he wouldn't know that you can't buy wishes, even with money like this.'

'I don't know,' said Pernickety. 'Maybe we're letting our imaginations run away with us.'

'Well, it looks as if somebody has struck it rich,' Fergal replied. 'And the thing is, how are we going to find out if we're right?'

'First,' Maggie suggested, 'we must find out more about the gold. Are you sure, Pernickety, you don't know the story about the schoolmaster?'

Pernickety shook his head.

'All right,' said Maggie. 'I think we'd better see you home. Maybe dad will tell us about it—and whether we can keep the £50.'

'You mean, whether *I* can keep it,' Fergal corrected her. 'Don't forget, I was the one that found it.'

'Maybe so,' said Maggie firmly, 'but it was our idea that you should go up there tonight, and I think we should share it.'

'So do I,' said Pernickety.

'Well, I don't know,' Fergal grumbled. 'We'll see.'

'Anyway,' Maggie continued, '£50 is an awful lot of money. There's plenty for all of us. Just imagine the things we could buy with it.'

'How are we going to say we found it?' asked Pernickety. 'We weren't supposed to be there tonight.'

They were outside his house now, and they stopped to discuss what they should do.

'You're right,' said Maggie, 'we can't very well rush in and tell our parents, can we?'

'Not now,' said Fergal. 'But we can in the morning. I mean, we don't have to say exactly when we found it.'

After some further discussion, they agreed that this was the best thing to do, and hardly able to contain their excitement, they parted company and went home to bed.

For what seemed a long time none of them could go to sleep. Not surprisingly, perhaps, shadowy figures kept flitting across their slumber, playing hide-and-seek with thoughts of all the things they could buy with £50.

Maggie looked across the breakfast table at Fergal. She could see he could hardly wait to tell the news of his good fortune, and when, a moment later, he spread the £50 note on the table, she thought her mother was going to faint.

Fergal himself reckoned his mother was even more surprised than the day she had brought her washing in from the line and a large brown beetle had fallen at her feet. A cockchafer beetle, Pernickety had said it was.

'Glory be to God,' she exclaimed, just as she had done at the sight of the large beetle, 'what's that?'

'It's a £50 note,' he told her.

'Where did you get it?' asked his father.

'Up at the Money Tree. It was in the water.'

His mother lifted the note to make sure he wasn't playing a trick on her with toy money, while his father put down his toast and came around the table to have a closer look, saying, 'That's an awful lot of money to leave at the Money Tree. I wonder who's it is?'

'That's what we were wondering,' said Maggie. 'We think there's something funny going on, and that it has something to do with the Wicklow gold.'

'The Wicklow gold? What's that got to do with it?'

'We don't know, dad,' said Fergal, 'but you must admit, it is funny. I mean, making a wish with a £50 note. What'll we do with it?'

'Well, you know,' said his mother, 'we always took the view that the coins in the Money Tree were sort of sacred.'

Fergal nodded. 'Anyway, most of them are bent.'

'But this is different,' continued his father. Getting to his feet, he put the bank-note into the pocket of his overalls and said, 'I think we'd better ask your grandfather.'

Pernickety arrived as they were going into the old man's cottage, and followed them in.

'What's this?' smiled the old man, 'a deputation?'

'Wait till you see this,' said Fergal.

His father took the £50 note out of his pocket and showed it to him.

'We found it up at the Money Tree,' Fergal explained.

The old man took the note and tested the texture of it between his finger and thumb. Then he turned it over and looked at the picture of Sir Christopher Wren.

'Is it a good one?' asked Pernickety.

'It seems all right to me,' said the old man.

'Can we keep it?' asked Fergal.

His mother was examining the note again. 'You know,' she said, 'it's the first time I ever saw a £50 note in my life. And it's Sterling too. It must be worth a good bit more in our money.'

'But can we keep it?' asked Fergal.

'Are you sure somebody didn't drop it?' inquired his grandfather.

'I don't see how they could have,' said Fergal. 'It was in the hole in the tree . . . in the water.'

'That's a funny place for anyone to leave it,' said his mother. 'Why should they put it in there?'

'I don't know,' Fergal replied, 'but we can't very well leave it there, can we? Somebody else is just going to take it.'

'That's true,' said his father. 'I think we should hold on to it. Your mother and I are going into town tomorrow morning. Maybe we should notify the guards that we found it—just in case some English visitor has lost it. Then, I suppose, we can lodge it in the bank. If nobody claims it, you can keep it—provided you share it. All right?'

In spite of what he had said about keeping it for himself, Fergal nodded. The others smiled.

'In the meantime,' said his mother, 'you'd better not say anything about it or somebody's sure to claim it.'

'While we're here,' said Maggie, 'would someone please tell us about the schoolmaster and the Wicklow gold.'

'Why?' asked her grandfather. 'Has Stumpy Joe struck it rich?'

'I don't know what he's done,' Maggie replied, 'but he's acting very strange. Did dad tell you we saw him in town? He just ignored us.'

'And he had a new pony,' said Fergal. 'It was lovely. I think he was trying to sell it.'

'Is that so?' said the old man. 'I hope it was better than the one he brought here.'

'You couldn't compare them,' Fergal told him. 'This one looked as if it had just won first prize at the show. Its mane and tail were plaited, and there wasn't a hair out of place.'

'And it was full of beans,' added Maggie. 'It was

prancing and kicking its heels up in great form.'

'Hmmm, I wonder what he did with the other one,' said the old man. 'I thought he was going prospecting.'

'So he was, and he seemed to know what he was talking about,' Pernickety recalled. 'He knew about the schoolmaster and everything.'

'You don't think he's struck it rich already?' asked Fergal.

His grandfather shook his head. 'It doesn't happen as simply as that.'

'Well somebody has struck it rich,' said Maggie, 'or they wouldn't be leaving £50 notes lying around.'

The old man smiled. 'So you think somebody has found the gold, or is making a big wish in the hope that they will find it?'

'Something like that,' said Maggie. 'Now grandad, will you please tell us about the schoolmaster. Where did he find the gold? And what happened to him?'

' I often heard it said he came from around Woodenbridge,' said her father.

'So he did,' said the old man. 'His name was Donaghoo.'

4 THE GREAT GOLD-RUSH

The old wall clock in the blacksmith's cottage was striking as they followed him into the parlour. It was a clock that always fascinated the children, because it belonged to another age, the era of the horse, long before they were born. The name of a company was printed around the top half of the face, and the word 'molliscorium' around the lower half, while on the bottom part of it, which housed the short pendulum, were the words 'compo' and 'embrocation'. These, their grandfather had told them, were all things that had been rubbed either into the harness, or into the horses themselves when they had sprains or other pains.

Fergal and Maggie could see their father looking up at the clock and thinking it was time he was going back out to work. However he was almost as curious as they were now, and so was their mother who seated herself on the edge of the small settee in a way that suggested she would wait a little while, but not too long as she had things to do.

Beneath a framed scroll that had been issued many years previously by the Worshipful Company of Farriers to certify that he was a registered shoeing smith, their grandfather rooted around in the drawer of a sideboard. Then finding at least one of the things he was looking for, he handed his son a small page from a magazine which the others could see bore the heading 'Gold Mines of County Wicklow.'

'What does it say, dad?' asked Fergal.

'It says there were mines on the slopes of Croghan Mountain near to the Wicklow-Wexford boundary.'

'That's right,' said the old man. 'They discovered gold in a river just south of Woodenbridge. It's called the Gold Mines River now. But go on.'

'It says that the total amount of gold recovered in modern times was estimated at between 7,000 and 9,000 ounces Troy.'

Fergal gave a soft whistle of surprise, and his father went on, 'But apparently that wasn't a lot compared with what was found in other countries.'

'What do they mean by modern times?' asked Pernickety, who was studiously trying to take it all in.

'I think they're talking about the last two hundred years or so, as distinct from ancient times when gold clasps and things were made for cloaks—you know, like the ones they have in the museum.'

'What else does it say?' asked Maggie.

Her father, who was reading down through the article to himself, replied, 'It says there were some substantial nuggets found, including one of over 20 ounces.'

'Imagine,' said her mother, thinking of the ounces and lbs she used in her baking.

'And that hardly a generation goes past,' he went on, 'without a reawakening of interest in the possibility of striking gold in Wicklow. The gold, it says, was found in alluvial deposits which implies that an original reef or vein existed which may still exist but is covered.'

'What does that mean?' asked Fergal.

'I think it means that it was washed down from somewhere,' said his mother, 'and that no one has found the original vein—the mother lode, I think they call it.'

'Does it say anything about the schoolmaster?' asked Maggie.

'Yes, here it is,' said her father. 'It says the original discovery was made by a school-teacher.'

The old man grunted and closed the drawer, saying, 'I have it, I have it.' He unfolded a page of an old newspaper, and going over to the light of the window told them, 'This says there was a gold-rush here in Wicklow shortly before the 1798 Rebellion, and that it started when a man crossing a stream that flows from Croghan Mountain found a piece of gold weighing about half an ounce.'

'The schoolmaster!' said Maggie.

The old man nodded. 'It says a schoolmaster by the name of Donaghoo—spelt with a double o—lived near the wooden bridge and that when school was over he would climb the hills and watch the stars, and then perhaps descend and count their numbers in the waters of the Avonmore or the Avonbeg.'

'How do they know he did that?' asked Pernickety sceptically.

'It was the way it was told by a man from the Avoca Valley who saw the gold rush. According to him, the schoolmaster was lean at first and his coat was threadbare, his tall thin figure and the brilliant expression of his sunken eyes having altogether a hungry look.'

The old man shifted slightly so that he could get more light from the window, and continued, 'It was said that the master blessed his neighbours in an unknown tongue, which the priest declared was not Latin, that he put stones into an iron pot when it would have been more seemly to have put potatoes in it, and watched them boiling until there was a noise and a crackling that made many tremble.'

'Maybe he was experimenting with rocks and things . . . to see if there was any gold in them,' suggested Fergal.

'Could be,' said his grandfather. 'Anyway, it seems he knew what he was doing, for one day he was gone. Where he went nobody knew, but it says here that within a month he returned. His threadbare coat was replaced by one of stout and shining cloth, his cheeks had come forth, and his eyes, having lost their haggard expression, retained only that restless and out-looking one that indicated either insanity or genius.'

'It was obvious to everyone,' the old man continued, 'that the schoolmaster had become very wealthy, but no one knew how. He wouldn't teach any more, but instead built the one-roomed schoolhouse into a lovely big home for himself and bought a farm. All the time he continued to ramble along the river banks, and it was said that when winter torrents poured down the hills, nothing could keep him indoors. Sometimes he would disappear again and return just as mysteriously as he had done the first time. Everybody, of course, was wondering what he was up to, and how he had become so wealthy. But over the years he kept his secret to himself and told nobody. Then he made a big mistake.'

'What was that?' asked Fergal.

'He fell in love with a girl called Mary Leahy.'

'And what was wrong with that?' asked Maggie.

'Nothing, except that she didn't love him. She already had a boy-friend. And just like Delilah who tormented Samson to find out where he got his strength, she tormented poor Donaghoo to tell her the secret of his wealth.'

'And did he tell her?' asked Pernickety.

'Don't you know he did! It says . . . where it is now. It says he told her the mountains had flung a tribute of gold into the streams, and that he had gathered it and sold it in Dublin.'

'What did she do then?' asked Fergal.

'According to the story she mocked him and told the secret to her real lover. But rather than see them become rich at his expense, he got his revenge by telling the secret of the gold to everyone, with the result that thousands flocked to the area to look for it.'

'And did they find it?' asked Maggie.

'They did. Gold dust and nuggets. It was so pure it was the custom in Dublin to put gold coins on to the opposite scale and give weight for weight.'

The old man folded the paper and put it back into the drawer. 'The great Wicklow gold-rush they called it, but it didn't last long. I suppose the Government wanted to get in on the act. They sent in the Kildare militia to take over the ground, but it was too late. Not a whole lot more was found, and when the Rebellion broke out the project was abandoned. They tried again afterwards, but it didn't come to much.'

'So they never found the mother lode,' said Maggie.

Her grandfather smiled. 'It doesn't look like it. But who knows. Stumpy Joe has a hungry sort of look in his eyes now that I come to think of it. Maybe he'll find it.'

'If someone hasn't beaten him to it,' said Fergal under his breath.

His mother got up to go, and holding up the £50 note to emphasize the point told him, 'Well, if anybody has struck it rich, it's yourselves, and it's going straight into the bank so you won't spend it.'

'And I'm not getting any richer standing here talking,' said his father. 'There's work to be done.'

When her parents had gone, Maggie said, 'Didn't granny used to have a gold nugget once?'

Her grandfather smiled. 'That's right. She found it when she was a child.'

'What happened to it?' asked Fergal.

'It was sold. Times were hard and we needed the money.'

'You said there was a curse on the gold,' said Maggie. 'Do you think that's why I was born with my leg like this?'

Her grandfather shook his head. 'Of course not, Maggie. You just have a weak leg, that's all. The doctor said it would come all right in time. No, all I meant was that the gold brought the schoolmaster riches, but it also became the curse of his life and brought him a lot of unhappiness. Gold often does that to people, you know.'

'Wasn't there gold-mining done somewhere in the Manor?' asked Fergal.

'That's right. Away over at the foot of the hills. But I don't know if they ever found any.'

'Could that be the real reason why the Arabs came here?' asked Maggie. 'You know, for the gold?'

'Sure they're already rich.'

'Well, we think they're up to something,' said Pernickety. 'And if it's not the gold, what is it?'

'It's your imagination, that's what it is,' smiled the old man. 'Now off with you and don't be giving the people up at the Manor any more trouble than they already have.'

However, he was wasting his time. They had already decided to pay a visit to the Manor that evening.

The Manor was a large period residence that was almost hidden from the rest of the community by mature beech woods. It was said to have been the proud boast of the family who built it that it could be seen from even the remotest corner of the estate, which ran to several thousand acres of the best grazing land in Wicklow. However, that was probably two or three hundred years ago, before the woods had matured. Now only its stacks of tall Tudor-style chimneys could be seen above the trees, giving it a degree of privacy never wished for by its original owners, but much appreciated by its inhabitants in more recent times.

The arrival of the Arabs had not brought much outward change to the Manor. Apart from the private twin-engined plane that soared in and out of a landing strip somewhere beyond the trees, and the comings and goings of the Customs officers who checked it, things were very much the same as they always had been. Several local people continued to work on the farm, looking after the sheep and horses, and in general it was treated with the respect normally accorded the big house. Those whose respect had turned to resentment had forecast that things would be different now that foreigners had taken it over, but life went on just as before as far as anyone could see. Few, however, including those who worked on the farm, had anything to do with the Manor itself, and Maggie, Fergal and Pernickety wondered what they would find as they now made their way towards it. They had gone up the road and cut in across the fields so as to avoid the main driveway, and were approaching the Manor from the direction of the airfield.

It was dusk, and the beech woods around the house were darkening into silhouettes against the sky. Beyond the hills the sun had set in a splash of orange and soon it would be the turn of the moon to light the sky.

Maggie was riding Star as she always did when it was too far to walk, and the boys were leading the pony by the bridle. 'So far so good,' she whispered.

Keeping just inside the trees, they could see that between them and another wood was the long flat field which the Arabs used as a runway. At one end, although they could hardly see it now, was a pole with a large orange sock on top to indicate the direction of the wind. At the other end, where they were heading, was the hangar where the plane was kept. They continued on and after some time the hangar, which was made of blackened sheets of corrugated iron, loomed up before them.

'I don't see the plane,' whispered Pernickety. 'It must be inside.'

'And I don't see anyone around,' said Maggie. 'Do you think we should have a look?'

'You stay here with Star,' Fergal told her. 'Come on, Pernickety, let's try and find out what they're up to.'

Crouching low, the two of them dashed across a patch of tarmac to the hangar. The large sliding doors were closed, but they found a small door around the side. It was slightly ajar, and hardly daring to breathe they slipped inside. They were immediately aware of the smell of aviation spirit and oil, and could feel the occasional oily patch on the concrete floor beneath their runners as they crept forward between some barrels.

Soon their eyes became accustomed to the blackness and they could make out the outline of the plane. It was much bigger than they had expected. The wings seemed to stretch from wall to wall, and the tail was so tall it was almost touching the roof. Tip-toeing forward, they stopped beside a large wooden box and looked up at the three propellor blades that sprouted from the shining steel nose-cone of the nearest engine. Beyond the engine they could see the window of the cockpit, and behind that a row of small circular windows for the passengers.

'How are we going to get up into it?' whispered Pernickety.

'Shussh,' warned Fergal, putting a finger to his lips. 'Listen!'

For a moment they could hear nothing except their own breathing. Then they became aware of a movement, and were horrified to see several shadowy figures standing around under the tail of the plane.

Pulling Pernickety back against the wooden box, Fergal whispered, 'They must be guarding it. Let's get out of here.'

They were about to slip back out when, to their dismay, they heard Star giving a snort outside and Maggie saying in a low voice, 'Where are you?' At the same time, they could just make out the men ducking down and running crouching towards the door.

Following as quickly as they dared, the two of them reached the door in time to see Maggie hobbling across the tarmac towards the pony, but before they could shout a warning, the men rushed from the shadows, scooped her up and carried her off into the darkness. A moment later, a car started up and drove off towards the house.

'They've caught Maggie!' cried Fergal. 'Come on! They must be taking her up to the Manor.'

Quickly Fergal mounted Star, and pulling Pernickety up behind him, galloped along the laneway after the car, the lights of which were bouncing about some distance ahead. As the shadow of the Manor loomed up, they could hear the car's wheels skidding on the gravel of the courtyard, but instead of stopping it swung to the left into the main driveway and headed for the front gate.

'Hold on, Pernickety,' cried Fergal, and urging Star to even greater speed, he took off down the driveway in hot pursuit. The lights of the car had disappeared now, and all they could hear in the darkness under the trees was the clippity-clop of Star's hooves and the splattering of mud on the rhododendron leaves as they passed.

Soon they were at the brow of the hill where the avenue emerged from the trees and ran down through the open fields to the road.

Seeing the car lights again, Fergal panted, 'There they are. I think they've stopped at the gate.'

Pernickety, however, could see nothing. He had both arms around Fergal's waist and was hanging on with all his might.

Fergal could now see the car's lights moving off and disappearing down the road. His heart sank, and a feeling of panic spread over him. Where, he wondered, could they be taking Maggie, and what was he going to tell his mother and father? Suddenly he heard a voice crying, 'Here I am, Fraggle. Is that you?' To his great relief, he could just make out his sister standing beside the gateway. Pulling Star to a stop, he jumped off and ran over to her. 'Are you all right, Maggie?' he inquired anxiously. 'What happened?'

Sliding to the ground, Pernickety brought Star over and handed Maggie the reins. 'Where did they go?' he asked.

'I think they must have gone around by the road to cut off whoever they thought might be with me.'

'But why did they take you?' asked Fergal.

'And why did they let you go?' asked Pernickety.

Maggie was still shaking. 'I don't know,' she replied. 'Maybe they decided to escort me out of the estate and leave it at that. The Sheik doesn't believe in half measures, does he?'

5 SEARCHING FOR STARS

Scared and all as they were, neither Maggie nor Fergal said anything next morning about what had happened at the Manor. Nor did Pernickety. They knew well that if they did they would get into trouble for snooping around the Sheik's plane and might never be allowed into the estate again. In any event, they had something else to talk about. Maggie's pony, Star, had disappeared from the stables during the night.

'And did you look after her properly when you came home?' asked their father. Somehow he suspected that they had been up to something when they had come in a bit of a sweat.

'Of course we did,' Maggie assured him. 'We put her in and rubbed her down. She was fine.'

'That's right,' said Fergal, 'but when we went out this morning Silver was still there and Star was gone.'

'Are you quite sure you shut the door properly?'

asked his mother.

Fergal nodded emphatically. 'The door was closed and everything was in order—honest.'

'The funny thing is,' said Maggie, 'her saddle's still there.'

'That's odd all right,' her father agreed. 'If anybody was going to steal her, you'd imagine they'd take the saddle too.'

'Well it's still there,' said Fergal.

'Maybe she just pushed against the door and it swung open,' said his mother. 'Why don't you have another look around while we're in town?'

'All right,' said Fergal. 'We'll have a look, but I don't see how the door could have swung open. I closed it myself last night.'

'Well, have another look anyway,' said his father. 'We'll mention it to the guards when we're in about the £50 note. You never know, they might spot her along the road somewhere.' He turned to go. 'And Fergal,' he added, 'stop picking that wart until your mother gets you something for it. You're only making it worse.'

When their parents had left for town, Maggie and Fergal called for Pernickety and asked him to help them in the search for Star.

'Where do you think we should look?' he asked.

'Well, we've already had a look around,' Fergal told him. 'She's not in any of our fields, and there's no sign of her on the road.'

'I think she's been stolen,' said Maggie. 'I mean, we closed her in properly and there's no way she could have opened that door herself.'

'But who would want to steal her?' asked Pernickety.

Maggie shrugged. 'Tinkers maybe.'

'Then why didn't they take the two of them, or the goats?'

'I don't know,' she admitted. 'It's very strange.'

They wondered about it for a moment, and Fergal said, 'I don't suppose Stumpy Joe would have anything to do with it?'

'What's that you say about Stumpy Joe?' asked his grandfather, who had just come into the yard.

'Star has disappeared,' Maggie told him, 'and Fergal was just wondering if he might have had anything to do with it.'

'But sure you said he had a pony the last time you saw him.'

'That's true,' said Fergal. 'I wonder what he did with the first one?'

'Probably sold it,' said the old man. 'Joe's a horse dealer at heart. Didn't you say he was trying to sell the new one too?'

'I think so,' said Maggie 'But you don't think he'd steal one of our ponies, do you? Not after what we did for him. I mean, shoeing his pony and giving him something to eat and everything.'

'Well, you must admit he was very interested in the ponies the day he was here,' Fergal reminded her.

'That's right,' said Pernickety. 'Particularly Star. He seemed to take a great fancy to her, didn't he?'

'I suppose he did,' said Maggie. 'Do you think we should try and find him?'

Her grandfather nodded. 'Why not? At least he might know if anybody's found her."

'But where are we going to look for him?' wondered Fergal. 'He said he was going prospecting and the next thing we saw him in town dealing in ponies.'

'Still, he seemed very set on this prospecting busi-ness,' said the old man. 'I'd say he won't be too far from the old mine workings. They're just beyond the river . . . you know, as you go up into the hills.'

Fergal gave Maggie and Pernickety a knowing look and said, 'But that's on the Sheik's land, isn't it?'

'And so what if it is!' replied his grandfather. 'That land up there's no use to anybody. He's hardly going to complain about you being on it.'

'I suppose not,' said Maggie. 'We can take Silver. It's a good bit up.'

When Silver was saddled, the other two helped Maggie on and headed up through the fields.

'What do you make of last night?' asked Pernickety.

'I don't know,' said Maggie. 'I'm still weak at the knees just thinking about it. I thought I was being kid-napped, you know.'

'Did you get a good look at them?' asked Fergal

Maggie shook her head. 'Not really. They had their faces blackened. But they seemed to be wearing some sort of jackets, you know, like the ones soldiers wear.'

'And did you see the way they moved?' Fergal recalled. 'Just like commandos.'

'The Sheik seems to have his own private army up there,' said Pernickety. 'Do you think they had guns, Maggie?'

'I didn't see any. But I wouldn't be surprised.'

'I still can't understand why they took you down to the gate instead of up to the Manor,' said Pernickety.

'I thought maybe they were going to take me straight to the garda-station,' said Maggie.

'Then why didn't they?' wondered Fergal.

'It's hard to say. I think maybe they changed their minds when they saw who I was.'

Pernickety was still puzzled. 'But how did they know who you were in the dark?'

'When one of them opened the door and got out to open the gate, the light came on inside the car. I suppose they must have seen then that I was from the forge. Anyway, they seemed surprised and just dumped me out on the driveway.'

'Did they say anything?' asked Fergal.

'No, they just let me out.'

'Well I think it's very strange,' said Pernickety. 'I mean, you'd think they'd check with the Sheik first, before taking you to the garda-station.'

'They seem to be able to do what they like,' said Fergal. ' I wonder were they afraid they'd get into trouble if the Sheik found out someone had been in around the plane?'

'And just decided to escort me out to the gate and say nothing about it?'

Fergal nodded. 'Yeh, why not?'

'But why should the Sheik have a guard on the plane in the first instance?' wondered Pernickety. 'Unless he has something to hide.'

'Well, somebody has been causing him a bit of trouble,' Maggie reminded him. 'They ran off his sheep, remember. And then there was the business of the slogans being sprayed on the wall. Maybe he was afraid they might sabotage his plane as well, and that must be very expensive.'

'But his own guards,' said Fergal. 'I mean, that's going a bit far. We thought maybe Ahmed had struck it rich with the gold, but I'm beginning to wonder if there's more to it than that.'

'You mean maybe the Sheik's mixed up in it too?' asked Maggie.

'Well, if Ahmed was up to something on the quiet, he wouldn't have a guard on the plane. The Sheik would have to know all about that.'

'It's true,' said Maggie. 'And anyway, if they have found gold somewhere on the estate, it would be a big job getting it out. It isn't something Ahmed could do on his own.'

'Unless,' said Pernickety, 'he was walking the hills like the schoolmaster, and found that the streams had flung forth a tribute of gold. Isn't that what your grandfather said happened to Donaghoo?'

'It's all very puzzling,' said Maggie. 'First the Sheik and his son come to visit the Money Tree and make a wish.'

'And Ahmed,' said Fergal.

Maggie nodded. 'And Ahmed. Then somebody who looks like Ahmed comes back and puts a £50 note in the water. And when we go up to the Manor to investigate, those men grab me and put me out. The very next day, Star disappears.'

'Do you think Star's disappearance could have something to do with it too?' asked Perickety.

'Well it's odd, isn't it?' said Maggie. 'I mean, nothing like this has ever happened before, and suddenly all these things happen at once.'

'And where does Stumpy Joe fit into it all?' wondered Fergal. 'You're forgetting about him.'

'I don't know,' said Maggie, 'but I think the sooner we talk to him the better.'

The sun was high in the sky now, and it was warm.

As they made their way through meadows that were aglow with buttercups, Pernickety kept stopping to clean his glasses and it became obvious to the others that he was beginning to tire.

'We'll never get anywhere at this rate,' said Fergal at last. 'Come on, Pernickety, up you go,' and he gave him a leg up behind Maggie.

Gradually the woods and the grazing fields fell away behind them and they were on rough hilly ground. Fergal led Silver between hummocks of grass and around soggy patches of seeping streams. Occasionally a snipe would break into flight with a screech, twist and turn, and disappear into the blue. They kept going and at long last found themselves looking down at the river. The water bubbled and sang its way across the stones, and sparkled brightly as each ripple caught the rays of the sun and flashed them back up into the sky. High above the river, swifts were circling in search of food.

Maggie shaded her eyes with her hand and scanned the area for any signs of Stumpy Joe. 'I can't see him anywhere,' she said at last.

'Well, let's go down and follow the river up a bit,' suggested Fergal. 'If he's looking for gold he's probably around here somewhere. The old mines are up there in the hills.'

'Okay,' said Maggie. 'Hold on, Pernickety. We're going down.'

Silver was accustomed to making her way across all sorts of terrain when she was out with the children, and she picked her way down through a network of sheep paths, as sure-footed as the sheep themselves. Emerging on to the grassy bank of the river, they made their way up along it, scanning the far side for any sign of Stumpy Joe. Being at the foot of the hills, the far bank was higher. It was scarred here and there with crevices of stones and reddish-coloured soil where the earth had either subsided or had been scooped out by cattle and sheep coming down to drink. Somehow they felt that was the sort of spot Stumpy Joe would pick to look for traces of gold.

It seemed for a while that they were mistaken, but when they rounded a bend there he was, squatting at the water's edge, peering into a large shallow pan.

'Hi ya, Joe,' shouted Maggie, and he responded with a smile and a wave of his cowboy hat.

'I don't see any sign of Star,' said Fergal.

Stumpy Joe, who was wearing wellingtons, waded across the river to meet them.

'How are you, Joe,' said Pernickety, sliding to the ground and adjusting his glasses.

'I'm rightly, Scholar,' he replied. 'How are you?' He placed the pan on the grass and helped Maggie to dismount. 'And what brings you all up here, might I ask?'

'We're looking for Star,' Maggie told him. 'She disappeared from the stables last night.'

'Star? Ah, you mean the pony with the wee white spot on her forehead?' They nodded, and he continued, 'A lovely animal she is too, but how come she got out?'

'Well, that's the point,' said Fergal. 'We're not sure if she got out or if somebody took her.'

'Ah now, hold on,' said Stumpy Joe. 'You don't think I had anything to do with it by any chance?'

'No, no, of course not,' said Fergal, anxious to reassure him.

'It's just that you seem to know a lot about ponies and things,' explained Maggie. 'We saw you in town with a new one.'

Stumpy Joe turned away and lifted the pan, saying, 'Oh, aye, the new one. Well, I must get back to work. I'll never strike it rich standin' here talkin'.'

'Then you haven't struck gold yet?' asked Fergal.

'If I had I wouldn't be standin' here now, would I? I'd be away somewhere spendin' it.'

'What happened your other pony?' asked Pernickety. 'The one you brought to the forge.'

Stumpy Joe took another panful of gravel and mud from the bed of the river, swirled it around and around, and allowed the dirty water to dribble over the edge. 'I sold it,' he said.

'And where did you get the new one?' asked Fergal.

'I bought it,' he replied.

They could see they weren't going to get much information out of him about his own ponies, whatever

about theirs, so Maggie said, 'We were just hoping you might keep an eye out for Star, you know, in case the tinkers have her.'

'Aye, I will,' he said. 'I will surely.'

'We also came to warn you,' said Fergal.

'Warn me? What about?'

'Grandad says there's a curse on the gold,' Maggie told him.

Stumpy Joe laughed. 'A curse? Well, don't worry about it. If I'm going to be cursed with riches, I'll chance it.'

'But look what happened the schoolmaster,' said Fergal.

'And then there are the Arabs,' added Pernickety.

'The Arabs? What about them, Scholar?'

'They own this land now,' Pernickety informed him.

'So what? They don't own the mineral rights.'

'How do you know they don't?' asked Fergal.

'I told you before. My grandfather prospected for gold in the Klondike. I prospected for it up in the Glens of Antrim, and I know about these things. The fact that you own the land doesn't mean you own the minerals that might be in it.'

'Well, you may be right, Joe,' said Maggie, hobbling over and sitting down on the bank beside him, 'but the Sheik's got his own security men and they don't mess about.'

'Ah, don't mind them,' said Stumpy Joe. 'Anyway, they wouldn't be runnin' around up here. It's the Sheik they'd be protectin', not lookin' over my shoulder to see what I've got in my pan.'

Fergal and Pernickey were looking over his shoulder now, and as they all gazed into the pan they saw him draining the muddy water out until only a few tiny pebbles were left in the groove beneath the rim. Then he poked the pebbles and remaining sediment with his finger to see if he could find any trace of gold.

'How can you find gold that way?' asked Fergal.

'That's the way it's done,' replied Stumpy Joe. He sat back, took off his cowboy hat and wiped the sweat from his brow with his sleeve. 'You see, the gold's heavier than anything else, so when you wash away the dirt it's left behind in the pan.'

'Is it really bright?' Pernickety asked him.

He nodded, and looking into the pebbles in the pan once more, said, 'It sparkles, just like the stars.'

'I wonder if that's what they meant when they said Donaghoo would count the stars in the waters of the Avonmore and Avonbeg?' wondered Maggie.

'Who?'

'The schoolmaster,' said Pernickety.

'Oh aye, Donaghoo. That was his name now you come to mention it.'

'Grandad said it was when he was counting the stars in the water that he found the gold,' explained Fergal.

'Is that a fact?'

Pernickety nodded. 'He found a nugget.'

'Aye it's here all right,' said Stumpy Joe, 'if you could only find it.' He scooped more mud and pebbles from the bed of the river.

'Did you find any in the Glens of Antrim?' asked Pernickety.

'Not really, but somebody must have, once upon a time. Why else did they call the mountain Slieve-anorra? It's from the Irish you know, *Slieve un Oir*. It means Mountain of Gold.'

'And where did you look for it?' asked Fergal.

'In the Glendun River, of course, where else?'

'Why do people always look for it in rivers?' asked Maggie.

'Because if there's gold in the hills, the river's bound to wash some of it down. It stands to reason. Then you go lookin' for the mother lode—the rock where it's comin' from.' He nodded towards the old mine workings and added, 'That's what they used to be diggin' for up there.'

Maggie plucked a small flower with bright blue petals and a white eye. She knew it was called speedwell, and that many years ago it used to be sewn on to the coats of travellers to protect them from harm and speed them on their way. She also thought that in some way it might be able to speed people in getting well, and she kept some in her bedroom whenever she could. 'If you did strike gold, what would you wish for?' she asked him.

'I wouldn't have to wish for anything,' he replied. 'Sure I'd have everything money could buy.'

'There are some things that money can't buy,' said Maggie.

'If there are,' said Stumpy Joe, 'I never heard of them.' He scanned the sediment in the pan once more for any traces of gold, and for a moment Maggie could see that her grandfather was right. Like Donaghoo, Stumpy Joe did have a hungry look in his eyes. She snipped off the head of the speedwell with her nail and watched it float down the river like a bright blue star until it disappeared.

'Come on, Maggie,' said Fergal, helping her to her feet. 'Let's go home.'

Having taken their leave of Stumpy Joe, Fergal and Pernickety found a more gentle path than the one they had come down, and led Silver back up to the ridge. Then, as they stopped to get their breath, Maggie sat back in the saddle and looked down at the small figure crouching over the pan at the river's edge. The water sparkled in the mid-day sun, and even as she shaded her eyes there was a flash of something else farther up among the hills. Straining her eyes, she could just make out the shape of a Land Rover on a dirt track that led down from the mountain road. Another movement brough her gaze back to the river, and she was startled to see four men running along the far bank towards them. They were wearing light green jackets pulled tight at the waist, and after her experience at the Manor, Maggie knew instinctively who they were.

'Look!' she cried. 'It's the Sheik's men!'

6   THE ARAB BOY

So intent was Stumpy Joe on panning for gold that he was unaware of the men who were now bearing down on him.

Fergal and Pernickety peeped over the ridge to see what was happening, but Maggie told them, 'Keep down,' and shouted at the top of her voice, 'Run Joe! Run ! '

Looking up, Stumpy Joe realized immediately what was happening, and dropping the pan on the grass took off as fast as his short legs could carry him.

'This way,' cried Maggie. 'Up here!'

'What are you doing?' asked Fergal. 'You're only drawing them on to us.'

'Be quiet,' said Maggie, 'and keep your head down.'

Stumpy Joe was half way up to the ridge now. Glancing around, he saw the men slithering down the bank and splashing across the river after him.

'Hurry!' urged Maggie.

A few moments later he scrambled up on to the ridge, and Maggie told him, 'Quick, get down, and give your hat and coat to Pernickety.'

'What for?' he asked.

'Don't ask questions. Hurry!'

Crouching down, he removed his hat and coat, and at Maggie's bidding Pernickety put them on.

'Pernickety's lighter than you are,' Maggie explained. 'Come on, Pernickety, get up behind me.' She reached down and pulled him up. The men were starting up the slope now. 'Keep down and follow me when you can,' she told the others. She swung Silver around, and with a flick of her heels galloped off along the ridge.

Down below the men stopped, and looking up saw what appeared to be Stumpy Joe and the girl getting away on the pony.

Up on the ridge, Stumpy Joe and Fergal were peering down through a clump of briars. They held their breath and hoped the ruse would work. It did, and when a few minutes later they saw the men going back across the river, they turned and ran for all they were worth.

Maggie and Pernickety were waiting for them in a hollow some distance away, and as they flung themselves down and lay panting in the long grass, Stumpy Joe was generous in his expression of thanks.

'That was fast thinkin' girl,' he gasped. Pernickety handed him back his hat and coat and he put them on. 'They nearly had me.'

'We told you the Sheik had his own security men,' said Maggie.

'Oh aye, the Sheik, the Sheik,' Stumpy Joe crawled back up to the top of the hollow, and, seeing no one, stood up and composed himself.

'You can't say we didn't warn you,' continued Pernickety.

'That you did,' said Stumpy Joe. 'And thanks very much.'

'Do you think maybe they've found the gold?' asked Fergal.

'The gold? What makes you think that?'

'Well,' said Fergal, 'they came from the direction of the old mines, didn't they?'

'Not at all,' said Stumpy Joe. 'Them fellas wouldn't know gold if it was starin' them in the face. They just don't like people being on their land, that's all. Foreigners are all the same.'

'The Sheik seems to be very nice really,' Maggie told him. 'We met him down at the Money Tree. Paddy Mac says his real name's Baracat.'

'Well I think he's a very dangerous man,' said Stumpy Joe. 'It's when them Eastern fellas are smilin' that you know they're up to somethin'.'

'We were thinking maybe they had started to work the old mines again,' said Maggie.

Stumpy Joe shook his head. 'Not a chance! I was up there and they haven't been worked for years.' He started to go, then turned around and added, 'If I see your pony, I'll let you know. And take my advice: Keep away from the mines. Places like that can be very dangerous.'

'Where are you going?' asked Maggie.

'Into town,' he told them. 'I think it's time I had somethin' to steady my nerves.'

There was a garda in the yard when they returned.

'What's up?' asked Fergal.

'Any sign of Star?' asked their father.

Maggie shook her head, and her father helped her off. 'Well,' he said, 'you'd better give Silver a rub down. She seems to have worked up a bit of a lather. I hope you weren't running her too hard.'

They didn't give him an answer, and fortunately he didn't seem to be expecting one. Instead he said, 'When you've done that I want you to show the guard where you found the £50 note.'

'And will we be able to keep it?' asked Fergal.

'Keep it is right,' said his mother. 'Sure isn't it a forgery !'

'A forgery!' said Fergal incredulously.

'How could it be a forgery?' asked Maggie.

Her mother shook her head. 'Don't ask me. But that's what the guard says.'

Pernickety looked up at the garda and asked him. 'How do you know it's a forgery?'

The garda opened the breast-pocket of his tunic, and taking out the £50 note held it up to the sun. 'It hasn't got the proper watermarks.'

'What are they?' asked Fergal.

The garda, who was still peering up at the note, explained, 'They're sort of shadowy outlines of people's heads and things that are put on notes to keep people from forging them. You can see them when you hold them up to the light.' He put the note back in his pocket. 'Mind you, it had me fooled. And the people at the bank said they wouldn't have given it a second look if we hadn't asked them to examine it. But there's no doubt about it, it's counterfeit.' He hooked his thumbs in under the buttons of the breast-pockets of his tunic and added, 'Now if you don't mind, I'd like to see where you found it.'

'I found it up at the Money Tree,' Fergal told him.

'Well, lead on.'

A short time later, the garda examined with great curiosity what he regarded as the scene of the crime. Nobody said anything, and the only sound was the crunching of his boots on the gravel as he walked around and around the Money Tree, viewing it from every possible angle. Then he looked at the hole in the trunk and dipped his hand in the water.

'It never dries up,' said Maggie.

'And I was just dipping in my hand to try and cure the wart on my knuckle,' Fergal told him.

The garda grunted, and sauntered casually back out through the gate to read the small plaque which had been put up by the Commissioners of Public Works declaring that the ruins were a national monument.

'Well,' asked Fergal at last, 'what do you think?'

'Have there been many visitors to the monastery this year?' asked the garda.

'Loads of them,' said Maggie.

'And what exactly do you mean by "loads" of them? Do you mean dozens, or hundreds?'

'Oh, hundreds of them,' added Maggie.

'And I take it they all visited the Money Tree as well?'

Maggie nodded. 'Some of them just come to see the Money Tree and make a wish.'

'It's amazing what some people will do with their money,' he remarked.

'How do you think the £50 note came to be in it?'

asked Pernickety.

The garda again hooked his thumbs into the breast-pockets of his tunic, drummed on the pockets with his fingers, and told him, 'The bank-note, or should I say the note which purported to be a bank-note, could have been left here by anybody.'

'Is that your conclusion then?' asked Pernickety.

The garda bent down and, looking into Pernickety's glasses, told him, 'That's my conclusion.'

'And what are you going to do with it?' asked Fergal.

'It will be kept as evidence,' replied the garda. He swelled out his chest, tapped his fingers on the pockets of his tunic again, and informed them, 'There'll have to be further investigations, of course. Naturally I'll have to notify the Fraud Squad up in Dublin, and get them to have a look at it.'

'Then what?' asked Maggie.

'Then,' he said, 'I may have to take statements from you, in case there are any proceedings.' With that, he strode off towards the forge, where he had left his bicycle, walking in a manner which suggested that he was deep in thought.

Fergal sat down and leaned back against the Money Tree. Like the others he was very disappointed that the £50 note had turned out to be worthless. Almost absent-mindedly, he watched a hoverfly buzzing around like a wasp before flying off at great speed. As if in a trance he remembered Pernickety telling him that hoverflies could vibrate their wings three hundred times a second. Getting up, he dipped his wart in the water again. 'What does he mean by "proceedings"?' he wondered.

Maggie, who was sitting on the wall with Pernickety,

told him, 'Court proceedings, I think.'

'How can there be court proceedings if he hasn't solved the case yet?' asked Pernickety.

'I suppose he means he may have to take statements from us whenever he has a suspect,' said Maggie. 'Which reminds me. I suppose we should really have told him the rest of it. You know, about seeing someone running away from here.'

'Ahmed,' said Fergal.

'If it was Ahmed who left the bank-note here,' said Pernickety, 'maybe it's not gold they're smuggling!'

'What then?' asked Fergal.

'Well, it was a forgery,' Pernickety reminded him.

'You mean they may be a gang of international forgers?' asked Maggie.

Pernickety nodded. 'Exactly!'

'But if that's the case, why should Ahmed leave one of the dud notes in the Money Tree?' asked Fergal.

'Maybe he's so nervous he's afraid they'll be found out,' said Maggie, 'and decided to make a wish.'

'And maybe,' added Pernickety, 'he got the forged money mixed up with his own. Maybe he didn't even realize the value of the note he was leaving.'

'That would explain a lot of things all right,' Fergal admitted. 'Like why they have a guard on the plane.'

'If only we could get a look inside it,' said Maggie, 'but I don't see how.'

'Unless we could make friends with the boy,' suggested Fergal. 'The only thing is, he didn't seem to be too friendly when he came here.'

'Still, I think that's a good idea,' said Maggie. 'Maybe we should try and make contact with him.'

'But how?' asked Pernickety. 'We can't go up to the

Manor again, that's for sure.'

'Who are you telling!' said Maggie. 'Still, we could keep an eye out for him. I wonder if he ever goes riding in the estate with his father?'

'Maybe we should take a canter around the near fields some morning and find out,' said Fergal. 'They can hardly object to that.'

Maggie wasn't so sure. 'You wouldn't know. We'd have to be very careful.'

Fergal nodded. 'But we could always say we were looking for Star. Are you game, Pernickety?'

Pernickety shrugged as if to say it didn't matter to him one way or the other. However, after all that had happened, it was obvious he wasn't too keen on the idea.

In the event, none of them was in any great hurry to go back into the estate. Once or twice they had a quick look around at the edge of it, but it was only when nothing happened that they decided to venture in a bit farther.

It was a warm sunny morning when they did so, and as they crossed the Manor fields once more they found that the sun had already dried the dew from the grass. Ahead of them they could see crows swirling around the beech woods in their thousands, while here and there among the flocks of sheep, magpies strutted about scavenging for food or whatever else might take their fancy. However, there was no sign of the Sheik's security men, and as Maggie, from her position astride Silver, assured the boys that the coast was clear, they began to relax and talk about something else.

'I don't like magpies,' Fergal remarked as he

watched them barely hopping out of the way of Silver's hooves. 'Grandad says they bring bad luck.'

'That's only an old superstition,' Pernickety told him.

'Superstition or not, grandad always tips his cap whenever he sees one. At least he used to. Now there are too many of them.'

'And they chase all the smaller birds away.' said Pernickety. 'There used to be loads of blackbirds' nests around our back garden, but the magpies wouldn't leave them alone.'

Suddenly Maggie, who was riding a short distance ahead, stopped and told them, 'There's the Arab boy over there. Now's our chance. Come on!'

Seeing the boy coming from the direction of a small beech wood, the others quickened their pace, but even as Maggie approached him Fergal spotted several familiar figures emerging from the trees and starting to run towards them. 'Look out, Maggie,' he warned, 'it's the Sheik's men again. Come on.'

As Maggie spurred Silver to a canter and circled around, she saw the boy tripping and falling flat on his face. 'Wait, Fergal,' she cried. 'We must help him.'

Fergal and Pernickety paused and threw a quick look back over their shoulder. The men were still a good distance from them. Hardly stopping to think, they ran back and helped the boy to his feet. At the same time, Maggie galloped around, herding the sheep in between them and the men. 'Run for it,' she cried. 'I'll delay them as long as I can.'

'Are you all right?' asked Fergal.

The boy nodded, and panted, 'Do not leave me. Please, do not leave me.'

Fergal looked at Pernickety and then at the Sheik's men. Thanks to Maggie the men were now knee-deep in a sea of sheep and were making very little progress through them. 'All right,' he said. 'Come on.'

Taking an arm each, Fergal and Pernickety helped the boy to hobble as fast as he could across the fields towards the monastery. Now and then they cast an anxious glance back, afraid that with every faltering step they took the men would catch up with them. To their surprise they saw them turn and run back into the woods.

Maggie circled around until she was sure the men weren't going to come after them from some other direction, and when she galloped up to the monastery she found the others sitting down, out of sight, around the Money Tree. Sliding to the ground, she took Silver into the ruins and left her where she wouldn't be seen. Back out at the gate, she gave a quick look around to make sure they weren't being followed, and sat down beside them.

'I must thank you for helping me up,' panted the boy.

'Well, you really don't deserve it,' Fergal replied.

'I do not understand,' said the boy.

'That's not the first time your father's security guards have run us off,' Maggie told him.

The boy looked at them, a puzzled expression on his face. 'Security guards? My father has no security guards!'

Fergal sat up with a start. 'Then who were those men who were chasing us?'

'I do not know,' said the boy. 'I thought they were chasing me. That is why I fell.'

The others looked at each other, bewildered.

'But it's us they've been chasing,' said Pernickety. 'And if they're not your father's men, who are they?'

The boy shook his head. 'I do not know, but I am most grateful that you came along when you did.' He paused for a moment, before adding, 'I really should be getting back. Monique will be worried, and I must tell my father what has happened.'

'Monique?' asked Maggie. 'Who's she?'

'My nurse.'

'Your nurse?' exclaimed Fergal.

'Yes, you must have seen her. She was with me when we visited the Money Tree.'

'We thought she was your mother,' said Maggie.

The boy shook his head. 'My mother died when I was small. Monique helps my aunt to look after me now. She comes from France, so she also helps me with my French.'

'You mean you speak French as well as English?' asked Fergal.

The boy nodded. 'But not as well as Arabic. I am afraid I do not yet know your Gaelic language, but perhaps I will learn it when I go to school here.'

The others looked at each other, embarrassed by their own lack of language.

'You're a strange boy,' said Fergal at last.

'I am not a boy,' was the astonishing reply. 'I am a girl. My name is Nadia.'

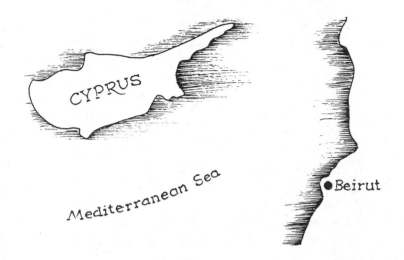

7   UNDER THE MONEY TREE

Fergal and Pernickety both jumped up as if they had suddenly found themselves sitting on red-hot coals. Then realizing that they might be seen by the men who had been chasing them, they eased themselves back down again.

'Does it embarrass you that I am a girl?' asked Nadia.

'No,' said Fergal. 'No, no, of course not.'

Maggie smiled, and as they all took stock of their new friend, they could see that she had indeed very feminine and very attractive features. In contrast to Pernickety's whitish hair, blue eyes and pale complexion, she had shiny black hair, large eyes that were as soft and dark as polished sloes, and sallow skin.

'It was the short hair,' explained Fergal. 'And the trousers. We though you were a boy. Sorry.'

'There is no need to apologize,' said Nadia. 'I am

not offended.'

'Why do you limp?' asked Maggie. The others were wondering the same thing, but Maggie felt she wouldn't mind her asking.

'My legs were injured in a car bomb explosion in Beirut,' she told her. 'Is that what happened to you? I read that you also have troubles in part of Ireland.'

Maggie shook her head. 'No, I just have a weakness in my leg, that's all. It's nothing serious.'

'Who was responsible?' asked Fergal. 'For the car bomb, I mean.'

Nadia shrugged. 'What difference does it make who was responsible? A bomb is a bomb to those it kills or injures. '

'Were you badly injured?' asked Pernickety, finally plucking up the courage to talk to her.

'Yes,' replied Nadia. 'I think I would have died if it had not been for my father. My legs were shattered, but he flew me to a hospital in France where specialists managed to save them. Sometimes I think I will never walk properly again, but my father has great faith. He is a very religious person, you know.'

'Is that why you came to the monastery?' asked Maggie. 'To pray?'

Nadia nodded, and Fergal said, 'But I didn't think Arabs would come here to pray. I mean, at a . . .'

'You mean a place of Christian worship? But we are Lebanese Christians.'

Once again the others felt very ignorant and embarrassed because of the assumptions they had made.

'And what about your pilot?' asked Pernickety. 'Is he very religious?'

Nadia smiled. 'Ahmed? He is in his own way I suppose, but he is not of our religion. He is a Muslim. He has been my father's pilot for many years—and his friend. Not even the fighting in Lebanon between Christians and Muslims could separate them.'

As they sat under the Money Tree talking, Maggie, Fergal and Pernickety tried to make sense of what Nadia had been telling them. With only a few well-spoken words, it seemed that she had demolished many of the assumptions they had made about the people at the Manor, and their theories about what was going on there. They had lots of things they wanted to say to her, lots of questions they wanted to ask. However, they didn't know her well enough yet. How could they tell her, for example, that whatever about her father, they suspected Ahmed was either an international gold smuggler or a forger? And they could hardly tell her they had been snooping around up at her father's private plane, at least not yet. Indeed, if they were going to tell her anything, they knew they would have to work their way around to it. They didn't want to hurt her feelings, especially after all she had been through.

'Why did your father come to Ireland?' asked Maggie.

'When the doctors in France had built up my legs with metal plates and things he took me to Cyprus to recuperate. I think he also wanted to be near Lebanon. But then he realized that it was still too dangerous in Beirut to return, so he decided to come to Ireland.'

'Did you not like Cyprus?' asked Pernickety.

'Oh I did, very much,' said Nadia. 'It has a lovely warm climate and I found the people very friendly.' She paused and added, 'They have a tree just like this.'

'Really,' said Maggie. 'A money tree?'

'Not a money tree,' Nadia told her. 'It is more like a holy tree or a healing tree. My father used to take me up into the Troodos Mountains. It was really beautiful. Sometimes we stayed overnight in the monastery of Kykko. It's like being on top of the world. In the morning we would get up early and go out and listen to the music of the goats.'

'Music of the goats?' said Fergal, thinking that when he milked Ginnie she bleated in a way that was anything but musical.

'Yes,' explained Nadia. 'You see, the hills are very steep and are covered with pine trees. So the shepherds of Kykko make bells and hang them around the necks of the goats—in case any of them go astray. The bells are made from iron and brass, and the mixture of the sound as the goats move among the valleys is very sweet. It is said that the tinkling of the bells keeps company to the shepherds in their lonely roaming and fills the mind with spiritual peace and serenity. Somehow I could not help feeling that it was like a mountain stream set to music.'

Having reflected on that memory for a moment, Nadia went on, 'The monastery is also very beautiful. It was built centuries ago to house an icon of Mary and the infant Jesus.'

'What's an icon?' asked Pernickety.

'A sort of picture,' she told him. 'According to tradition it was painted by St. Luke when Mary was still alive, and there is a long tradition of healing associated with it. It is said that once, when there was a fire at the monastery, a man who was paralysed was made well so that he could save himself and rescue the holy icon. He placed it in a pine tree nearby, and the flames never reached it.'

'Is that the Healing Tree?' asked Maggie.

Nadia shook her head. 'That was many many years ago. The Healing Tree is small, a golden oak, I think. It is on a hill above the monastery. People do not put money into it the way you do here. They hang little cloths on it, like a scarf, or a stocking or part of a shirt, depending on where they have the illness, and they say prayers for their recovery. We prayed at it many times.'

When the others didn't say anything, Nadia continued, 'Tradition has it that the monastery was built on a spot where a strange bird sang:

> *'Kykkou, Kykkou, Kykko's hill,*
> *A monastery the site shall fill.*
> *A golden girl shall enter in,*
> *And never shall come out again.'*

'What does that mean?' asked Fergal.

'I do not know,' Nadia confessed. 'Perhaps the holy icon. But I came away from it feeling almost like a different person; peaceful somehow, and more hopeful.'

Promising herself that she must find out more about their own monastery, Maggie asked her gently again, 'And why did you come to Ireland?'

'Cyprus is a small island, and Turkish soldiers have taken over half of it. My father wanted to buy much land with plenty of grass. I think he is planning to breed horses.'

'He must have plenty of money,' said Fergal, 'but then he would have, being an oil sheik.'

Nadia laughed. 'My father is not in the oil business. He is a financier. Beirut, you know, was the financial centre of the Middle East before all the trouble broke out. He deals in money, not oil, and he is not a sheik.'

'Nadia,' said Maggie, 'we think there is something very odd going on here, and that somehow it involves the Manor. If we tell you what has happened and what we think, do you promise you will not be offended?'

Nadia smiled. 'Of course I will not be offended.'

'Good,' said Maggie, 'because we want to be your friend, and we need your help.'

Bit by bit they told Nadia about some of the strange things that had happened since the day Stumpy Joe and then she and her father had called—how someone who looked like her father's pilot had left the counterfeit £50 note at the Money Tree; how someone had stolen Star; about the old gold-mines that were on her father's land; how the same men who had chased her had chased Stumpy Joe and themselves over at the mines; and how they suspected something very funny was going on at the Manor. However, they didn't tell her that the first time they saw the men was up at the hangar, as they didn't want her to know that they had been snooping around.

'But we have not been doing any work at the gold-mines,' said Nadia. 'I doubt if my father even knows that they exist. As for forgeries, he makes all the money he needs from dealing in real money.'

'We're not really suggesting that your father would know anything about it,' Maggie assured her, 'but what about your pilot? We're sure it was him we saw the night we found the forged note.'

'Ahmed is very loyal to my father,' said Nadia. 'He would not use the plane for a wrong purpose, if that is what you are thinking.'

'And what about those men who chased us?' said Fergal. 'If they're not your father's guards, who are they?'

Nadia shook her head.

'And if they were chasing you today,' said Pernickety, 'why were they chasing us over at the mines?'

'Unless it was Stumpy Joe they were after,' said Maggie. 'But why should they be after him?'

'It is all very strange,' Nadia agreed. 'Unless they are trying to scare us. Do you think perhaps it was the same people who chased the sheep and painted the slogans on the walls?'

'It's possible, I suppose,' said Maggie, 'but somehow I don't think so. I still think it's got something to do with Ahmed.'

'Whatever it is, I must tell my father,' said Nadia. 'Now I really must go. Monique will be wondering where I've got to.'

Fergal peeped over the wall to make sure the coast was clear. 'We haven't told our parents yet,' he said. 'We were afraid we wouldn't be allowed on to the Manor land again.'

'And maybe you shouldn't tell your father either,' Maggie suggested. 'At least, not yet.'

'Why not?' asked Nadia.

'Because,' said Pernickety, 'your father would go straight to Ahmed. And if Ahmed *is* mixed up in something, we'll never find out what it is.'

Nadia was quiet for a moment, and they could see she was considering what was the best thing to do. 'But this is a very serious matter,' she said at last. 'I cannot keep it from my father for long.'

'Then you will help us?' said Maggie.

'Only if it will help Ahmed,' replied Nadia. 'But what can we do?'

'It must be something to do with the plane,' said Fergal.

'Why do you say that?' asked Nadia.

Not wishing to tell her that they had already been up at the plane, Fergal said, 'Because Ahmed is the one who's acting strangely, and he's the one who flies it.'

'Do you think we could have a look at it?' asked Maggie.

Nadia struggled to get to her feet and Fergal and Pernickety helped her. ' I do not see why not,' she said. 'I am sure my father would have no objection, but it is a long way back and I think we should go by the main gate. It might be safer.'

Maggie led Silver out of the monastery, and feeling not quite so handicapped as before, managed to climb up into the saddle unaided. 'Come on,' she smiled. 'Get up behind me. They can walk.'

The boys helped Nadia up and they all set off for the Manor. This time they went along by the road and up the front avenue. They were a bit uneasy when they came to the wooded part of the avenue, especially as the rhododendron bushes could have been hiding someone, but no one bothered them and they arrived safely at the Manor a short time later.

Monique met them on the steps of the Manor, and seeing that Nadia's clothes were dirty, exclaimed, 'Mon Dieu! What has happened?'

The question was repeated by Mr. Baracat who had also appeared at the door.

'I fell,' said Nadia, lowering her eyes with the embarrassment of not telling the whole truth. 'My friends helped me and gave me a ride back.'

'Ah, the children of the forge,' said her father. 'Thank you.'

'They wondered if they could see the plane,' said Nadia.

'Well, I think they have earned that much,' said Mr Baracat. 'As soon as you have changed you can take them over to the hangar. I think Ahmed is there. Tell him I said it is all right.'

The others declined Mr. Baracat's invitation to go in and wait for Nadia, and seeing that they were somewhat uncomfortable at the prospect, he smiled and said, 'As you wish.' Then he followed Nadia and Monique into the house.

When Nadia re-emerged, she had changed into a completely new outfit. Monique was more relaxed now, and Nadia introduced her new friends by name.

Monique smiled, saying, 'Comment allez-vous, mes enfants?'

'I am going to show them the plane now,' Nadia told her.

'Very well, but be careful,' said Monique, as she helped her up behind Maggie again.

Nadia guided them along a wooded path until they came to the hangar. The plane was now parked on the patch of tarmac outside, and Ahmed and a mechanic were standing in front of it discussing some problem or other.

'Ahmed,' cried Nadia. 'Ahmed.'

'Remember now,' whispered Fergal, 'don't say anything until we find out what's going on.'

Seeing them, Ahmed broke off his conversation and hurried over. He seemed to be very fond of Nadia, and reached up and helped her to the ground. At the same time, he gently admonished her for bringing visitors to the hangar, saying, 'You know your father has forbidden it.'

'I know, Ahmed,' said Nadia. 'But these are special visitors, and father says it is all right. These are the children of the forge. I fell and they brought me back.'

Ahmed took out his handkerchief and wiped his bald head. 'My humble apologies,' he said with a slight bow. 'This way please.'

Taking them over to the plane, he proceeded to show them around it, pointing out certain features as he went.

'Is it a jet?' asked Fergal.

'How can it be a jet if it's got propellors,' said Pernickety.

'It is a twin-turbo prop,' Ahmed told them, and

looking up at one of the engines he proudly explained, 'It is a jet engine with a propellor. It is much lighter than an ordinary piston engine but more powerful. That is why it can fly higher and faster than an ordinary plane.'

Maggie was looking at one of the wheels, which were bulb shaped, and asked, 'Why are the wheels like that?'

'Because we take off from grass,' Ahmed told her. 'These are high flotation wheels. They keep us from sinking in the soft ground.'

'Our runway is over 1,000 metres long,' said Nadia.

'How far can it fly?' asked Pernickety.

'That depends on how many passengers we want to carry,' said Ahmed, 'and how fast we want to go.'

'Come,' said Nadia. 'You must see inside.'

'But, Nadia,' protested Ahmed. 'I am very busy. I think perhaps they have seen enough.'

'You can continue with your work, Ahmed,' she replied. 'I will show them. Father said I could.'

They followed Nadia around to the steps where she took a firm grip of the rail and pulled herself up, one step at a time. The boys offered to help, but she indicated that she was able to manage on her own. Seeing what she could do, Maggie followed her up unaided, and when they had gone inside the boys climbed in after them.

Ahmed remained at the foot of the steps for a few moments, and mopping the sweat from his brow, walked away.

Maggie peered out of one of the circular windows and remarked, 'Ahmed doesn't seem very happy about us being here.'

'Maybe he's afraid we'll find whatever he's trying to

smuggle out of the country,' said Fergal.

'I cannot imagine Ahmed being involved in anything like that,' said Nadia. 'But if you feel someone is using the plane for smuggling, we must find out who it is.'

The plane was furnished in a most luxurious fashion. The seat coverings, curtains and carpet were a rich royal blue, and even the top of the toilet was padded so that it served as an extra seat.

Nadia opened a curtain at the back, saying, 'This is the cargo hold. We keep our luggage in here.'

The others squeezed in beside her and she explained that the two seats which were folded up against the sides could be taken out to make more room.

There was no sign of any cargo, and Pernickety asked, 'Where else could something be hidden?'

Nadia hobbled back up the aisle and sat down on one of the high-backed passenger seats. The others followed and did likewise. 'There are a lot of panels under the carpet,' she told them. Reaching down, she pulled back the carpet between the seats and prised up a panel from the floor. However, all they could see were cables.

Fergal and Pernickety were looking through into the cockpit at the rows and rows of dials and switches when Maggie, who was helping Nadia to put the carpet back into place, remarked, 'Somebody's been in here with muddy shoes !'

'Well, it's not me,' said Fergal, who was always in trouble at home for not cleaning his feet on the mat before going in.

'I didn't say it was you,' replied Maggie. 'Anyway, it's dried out, so it couldn't have been any of us.'

'Do not worry,' said Nadia. 'I will see that it is

cleaned. But it is most unusual. Ahmed is so particular about such things.'

'It's red clay too,' observed Fergal. 'I wonder where that could have come from?'

'That type of clay was on our runners when we came back from the river,' Pernickety recalled. 'I remember, because my mother gave out to me about it.'

'You're right,' said Maggie.

'So whoever was here must have been up near the old mine workings,' said Fergal.

'But who?' asked Nadia.

'Those men,' whispered Fergal. 'Or Ahmed . . .'

Ahmed, who had just put his head in around the doorway, came crouching along the aisle and sat down beside them. He wiped his brow once more, and said, 'Forgive me, Nadia, but I could not help overhearing your friends saying something about the old mines. I must ask you to keep away from them. It is very dangerous for you there, and I have promised your father I will try and look after you.'

'But if you are in some sort of trouble,' said Nadia, 'perhaps we can help you.'

Ahmed shook his head and told her, 'No, my little one. I can handle it. It is your safety that is important. Just stay close to the Manor and you will be all right.'

'So you are in trouble,' said Nadia.

'It is nothing that I cannot handle myself,' Ahmed assured her. 'But you must stay away from the mines, or your life may be in danger.'

'Then you must tell father,' said Nadia, 'and the police.'

'If I tell the police, *my* life will be in danger,' replied Ahmed.

'Then how can we help you?' asked Nadia.

'You can help me by saying nothing of what I have told you. Stay close to home and leave it to me.'

'I still think you should tell father,' said Nadia, 'whatever it is.'

'Please Nadia,' Ahmed implored. 'Trust me. I will tell your father just as soon as I can, I promise.'

When she didn't reply, Ahmed took out his hand-kerchief and began mopping the sweat from his fore-head once more. 'Very well,' she said at last. 'You know best.'

Greatly relieved, Ahmed helped her to her feet, and she hugged him affectionately before making her way back out of the plane.

'What are you going to do?' asked Maggie as they went back through the woods to the Manor.

'We must go to the mines,' replied Nadia. 'We must find out what is going on.'

'You told Ahmed you wouldn't,' said Fergal.

Nadia, who was very precise in her use of English, corrected him. 'I told him I would not tell my father. I did not say I would not go to the mines.'

'But if Ahmed is right, you could be putting yourself in danger,' said Pernickety. 'We all could.'

'Well, whatever is going on,' said Nadia, 'I think the answer must be at the mines.'

'I think you're right,' said Maggie. 'Maybe those men were chasing us because we were getting too close to them.'

'And what happens if we run into them again?' asked Fergal. 'We only have one pony now that Star has gone.'

Nadia smiled. 'I have a pony. His name is Cedar.

Come, I will show you.'

'What will you tell your father?' asked Maggie.

'The same thing that you will tell yours. We are going to look for Star.'

Having taken their leave of Nadia, the others made their way down towards the forge.

'I wonder who those men are?' said Fergal. 'And how did Ahmed get mixed up with them?'

'I don't know,' said Maggie, 'but they seem very anxious to keep us off the Sheik's land, whatever they're doing.'

'What I don't understand,' said Pernickety, 'is, if they're not the Sheik's men, why did they grab you up at the hangar, Maggie, and then drop you off at the gate? That's the funny part of it.'

Maggie shook her head. 'I don't know. I can't understand that either. But you know, I've a feeling we should have told Nadia about it.'

'I know what you mean,' said Fergal. 'But, if we had, she mightn't have forgiven us for snooping around up at the plane.'

'And once she heard those men had been at the plane, she'd have gone straight to her father,' said Pernickety. 'He'd have brought in the guards, and that would have been the end of it.'

'I suppose you're right,' Maggie added. 'Still, I wonder if we should have told her? I just hope we don't run into those men again over at the mines.'

'Well, if we do,' Fergal assured her, 'they won't have a hope of catching us—not on two ponies.'

8   ALL THAT GLITTERS

The morning mist had only begun to lift from the lower fields as Fergal and Pernickety walked up the winding avenue of the Manor with Silver and Maggie. They reckoned it wouldn't be many more weeks until such a mist would lift to reveal a good crop of mushrooms and they would be out picking them. This morning, however, they were looking for something else.

Half way up they met Ahmed driving out, and pulled in to the side to let him past. They were amused to see him hunched up in a fawn duffle coat and guessed he was still having a problem adjusting to the Irish weather. He waved, in an agitated sort of way, but didn't stop, and they were glad as they were afraid he might ask them where they were going.

When they arrived at the Manor, Nadia was already in the saddle, and Monique watched from the doorway

100

as Mr. Baracat tightened the girth to make sure the saddle was secure. He bade them good morning and warned his daughter to be careful.

'I will, father,' she promised, and off they went.

Cedar wasn't as tall as Silver, but was black and bright and beautiful.

'Why did you call him Cedar?' asked Maggie.

'After the cedars of Lebanon, of course. The cedar tree is our national emblem.'

When they had gone far enough to be out of sight of the Manor, Fergal climbed up behind Maggie, and Pernickety got on behind Nadia.

'We met Ahmed on the way up,' said Maggie. 'I wonder where he was going?'

'I do not know,' replied Nadia. 'I kept out of his way in case he might ask me to promise not to go near the mines.'

'You didn't mention anything to your father then?' asked Maggie.

Nadia shook her head. 'No. But I feel guilty that I have deceived him. I must tell him as soon as I can and hope that he will forgive me.'

'And what about your aunt?' asked Fergal. 'Do you think she'll mind?'

'Of course! She already thinks I get too much freedom.'

'How come we never see her?' asked Fergal.

'She still prefers the old ways and does not show herself much. However, father says that now I am living in Europe I must learn to be a European. I hope I have not betrayed his trust.'

'I know how you feel,' said Maggie. 'But what else could we do? If we said we were going, we wouldn't be allowed. And Ahmed did say it would put his life in danger if we told.'

'I hope we're doing the right thing,' said Pernickety.

'Better be careful,' teased Fergal, 'in case Donaghoo's ghost jumps up out of the mines and grabs you.'

Maggie gave her brother a dig in the ribs with her elbow, and said, 'Would you give over, Fraggle. We'll see how smart you are when we get there. Anyway, it's not Donaghoo's ghost you should be worrying about. Keep your eyes skinned for those men.'

They continued on towards the hills, and Fergal said, 'I wonder what Stumpy Joe has got to do with all this? He said the very same thing to us as Ahmed.'

'That's right,' said Pernickety. 'He told us to keep away from the mines too. He said they could be very dangerous.'

'Maybe he knows more than he's telling,' said Maggie. 'I wonder if he knows anything about Star? It's funny how she should disappear like that. Somehow I think it's all part and parcel of whatever's going on.'

'What do you mean when you say "part and parcel"?' asked Nadia.

Maggie smiled. 'It's just a saying we have. I suppose it just means that it's part of the same thing.'

'You mean part of the same parcel?'

'Yes, I suppose so.'

'If we're going to find out what's going on at the mines,' said Fergal, 'we can't just ride up to them.'

'And we'd better avoid the mountain streams,' said Pernickety. 'The snipe will give the game away before we get within a mile of them. Maybe that's how they spotted us the last time.'

'You could be right,' said Maggie. 'Maybe if we went down to the river sooner and followed it, we could get fairly close without being noticed.'

They all agreed that this was the best thing to do, even though it would take them longer to get there. They were also half hoping they might come across Stumpy Joe again, and maybe even enlist his help. However, there was no sign of him.

The only crouching figure they came upon was a grey heron standing motionless in the water as it scanned the shallows for flashes of silver that would indicate the presence of fish. It rose into the air as they approached and flew slowly up-river in search of a quieter place.

They were now at the bend in the river where they had found Stumpy Joe panning for gold. The river, they could see, was deserted. They were well shielded from the mines by the high bank on the far side, so looping the reins over the lower branches of an alder tree they left the ponies and went forward on foot.

'We didn't come up as far as here with Silver the last time, sure we didn't?' whispered Maggie.

'No,' replied Fergal. 'Why?'

Maggie pointed to shoe marks in the mud. 'There's been another pony up here. I wonder if it was Star?'

Fergal tip-toed across several large stones in the river and examined a muddy slope on the far side. 'The tracks are over here too,' he told them.

With a helping hand from Fergal and Pernickety, Maggie and Nadia managed to cross over.

'Do you still want to go on?' asked Fergal.

Nadia nodded, and asked, 'Are the mines far?'

Fergal scrambled up the slope, and peering over the top told her, 'They're just over there, and there's no one around. Come on.'

With Fergal pulling and Pernickety pushing, Nadia and Maggie eventually succeeded in reaching the top. They could see that the tracks of the pony led straight for the old mine workings, and they hurried over as fast as they could.

In days gone by, someone had decided that if Donaghoo could find gold on the slopes of Croghan Mountain, it might be worthwhile digging for it here too. Whether or not they had found it no one seemed to know, but there were still various tunnels and caves to testify to the fact that part of the hill had been scooped out and, presumably, sluiced down into the river to see if it contained any gold.

'I wish we had a torch,' said Fergal. He paused a short distance inside until their eyes adjusted to the darkness. 'Anyway, there's nothing we can do about it now. Hold on to me and watch your step.'

Inch by inch they crept forward, holding on to each other with one hand, and feeling their way along the wall with the other.

'Listen,' Fergal whispered.

'What is it?' asked Pernickety, from the rear.

'Some sort of engine I think. And it seems to be getting brighter.'

The noise was becoming louder now, and soon they saw that a part of the tunnel was illuminated by an electric light.

'What's the engine doing?' asked Maggie.

'Must be a generator,' said Fergal. 'For the light.'

Tip-toeing forward, they saw that the entrance to a

large side-chamber had been partitioned off, almost as if someone had used it at some stage as a stable or a sort of shed. The door was open, and they ventured in.

'It's full of machinery,' gasped Fergal.

'Printing machines,' whispered Nadia.

'And paper,' said Maggie, raising her voice now that she saw there was nobody there. She lifted a large ball of crumpled paper from the top of one of the machines and opened it up. 'Look, it's printed all over with bank-notes!'

'Dollars,' put in Nadia. 'They are very valuable in Lebanon.'

Fergal and Pernickety were examining a collection of tins and jars in a corner.

'Ink,' observed Pernickety. 'I've never seen so many colours.'

Some of the tins had been left open and they could see that the ink at the bottom had hardened.

The girls were examining a pile of crumpled papers that had been discarded in another corner. On some of the sheets the notes were blurred; on others they had been printed crooked.

'They must have been practising,' said Maggie. 'And they've been printing other things besides dollars. Look, they've also been making English £50 notes.'

'Just like the one I found at the Money Tree,' said Fergal.

'There are very few sheets of paper left,' Nadia observed. 'I hope we are not too late.'

'These ones have been printed,' said Maggie, 'but they haven't been cut yet.'

'And the printing plates are still here,' observed Pernickety, peering into one of the machines. 'There

are gadgets to put the numbers on the notes and everything.'

Now as they wondered where the forgers were, there
was a grunting noise and a sort of shuffle from beyond
another door. Frightened, they all hurried out into the
passageway. No one followed them, and they stopped
and listened.

'There it is again,' whispered Maggie. 'You don't
suppose it could be Star by any chance?'

'Well, we did see pony tracks outside,' said Fergal.
'Wait here, I'll have a look.'

'Be careful, Fraggle,' warned Maggie, and they
watched as he tip-toed across to the other door,
pushed it open and looked in.

'It's Stumpy Joe!' he cried and disappeared inside.
The others followed and found him kneeling beside
the little prospector who was lying on the floor, bound
and gagged.

'Here, give me a hand,' said Fergal.

Pernickety dropped down beside him and helped to untie the knots.

When Stumpy Joe was free, he scrambled to his feet, picked up his cowboy hat and planted it firmly on his head. 'You shouldn't have come here,' he panted. 'I warned you it was dangerous.'

They followed him out to the printing machines and Maggie asked him, 'But why did *you* come here?'

'That's different,' he replied. 'If somebody was back in the mines I wanted to know if they had struck it rich.'

'Somebody has struck it rich,' remarked Fergal, referring to the money.

'All that glitters is not gold,' said Stumpy Joe. 'Isn't it dud money?'

'Who tied you up?' asked Nadia.

'The fellas that are makin' this stuff, who else?'

'This is our friend Nadia,' said Maggie. 'She's from the Manor. We discovered that Ahmed, that's their pilot, is mixed up in this somehow.'

'Who are they anyway?' asked Pernickety.

'Ah well now, I wouldn't be knowin' that, Scholar,' replied Stumpy Joe.

Suddenly his voice seemed agitated, and he reached out and pulled them closer to him in a protective sort of way. Looking around, they were startled to see several men standing watching them. They wore black woollen masks and only their eyes, noses and mouths could be seen. Even so, it was obvious from the way they were dressed that they were the men who had been chasing them. It was also obvious that they were smiling, and when they spoke it was with Irish accents.

'This solves all our problems,' said one of them.

Another nodded. 'Ahmed has no option now. He'll have to do the job for us.'

'Right,' said the first. 'We'll let him know we've got the girl.'

'So that's it!' exclaimed Maggie.

Immediately one of the men drew a revolver from his jacket pocket, and ordered them to be quiet.

Frightened, Maggie and the others took a step back.

'This is kidnapping,' protested Stumpy Joe. 'Let the children go.'

'Kidnapping?' said the first man. 'Sure how could it be kidnapping? They came here of their own free will, didn't they?'

'Then let them go,' pleaded Stumpy Joe.

'Not on your life,' said the man with the gun. 'Ahmed was a bit reluctant to do a job for us, but somehow I think he's going to change his mind.' Motioning with the gun, he ordered them back into the room where Stumpy Joe had been tied up, and closed the door.

Maggie placed her hands on Nadia's shoulders, saying, 'I'm sorry, Nadia. I'm sorry that this has happened. I mean, after all you've been through.'

Fergal explained to Stumpy Joe about Nadia's legs.

'You have no need to apologize for the action of others,' said Nadia. 'And anyway, you must not worry about me. I will be all right. It is Ahmed I am worried about. If he is caught smuggling forged money in his plane he will be in much trouble.'

'Don't worry your pretty wee head about it,' said Stumpy Joe. 'Your father's a big man in the business world from what I hear. He'll look after it.'

'But he does not know anything about it,' explained

Nadia. 'I am afraid I did not tell him. I deceived him.'

'Well, if that's deceiving him, then we deceived you,' said Maggie. 'You see, we saw those men at the plane.'

'When?' asked Nadia.

Maggie related what had happened the night they had grabbed her outside the hangar, and added, 'It didn't occur to me before, but they must have thought I was you. I suppose we should have told you, but we were afraid to. We didn't want you to know we had been snooping. Sorry.'

If Nadia was disappointed in them, she didn't show it, saying simply, 'I'm sure you did what you thought was best.'

'I'm sure you all had good reason for doin' what you did,' said Stumpy Joe. 'Anyway, there's nothin' we can do about it now, so you might as well sit down and make yourself comfortable. And don't mind them fellas out there, Nadia. You're among friends in here.'

'But what are we going to do?' asked Nadia anxiously. 'How are we going to get out of here?'

'That's a good question,' said Stumpy Joe, 'and I wish I had the answer.'

9   A RACE AGAINST TIME

The place where they were imprisoned had obviously been used for tea-breaks by whoever had done the printing. Unwashed cups, spoons, used tea-bags, a packet of sugar and a half-empty bottle of milk littered a table in the middle of the floor, and there were some wooden chairs.

Stumpy Joe tip-toed over to the door, and taking off his hat squinted through a crack in the wood. When he returned he sat down beside them saying, 'They've left one fella out in the tunnel to keep an eye on us, but I don't think he can hear us, not with the noise of the generator, so you can talk away.'

'What have you got to do with all this?' asked Maggie. 'And where's Star? Have they got her?'

'Now you have it, girl,' said Stumpy Joe. 'From what I can gather they were afraid to drive back up on to the road and in through the town with the money in case

110

they might be stopped. So they stole Star to carry it across country to the plane.'

'Is she all right?' asked Maggie.

'And why not? It's my guess the money's already on the plane, so they've probably turned her loose.'

'Is your father due to fly to Lebanon soon?' asked Pernickety.

'No,' Nadia told him, 'but Ahmed is.'

'When?' asked Fergal.

'Just as soon as the mechanic has finished checking the plane. Ahmed will take it on a short test flight, probably as far as Dublin airport. Then he will be ready to go. That is what he normally does.'

'If they have put the money on board,' asked Pernickety, 'where do you think they've hidden it?'

Nadia shrugged. 'There are so many hiding-places, it is difficult to say. But if there is much of it, it is probably in the hell-hole.'

'The hell-hole? What's that?' asked Fergal.

'It's the space behind the cargo hold. You can reach up into it from underneath. Our mechanic calls it the hell-hole.'

'And is it far to Lebanon?' asked Stumpy Joe.

Nadia nodded. 'We do it in stages.'

'But, Joe,' said Maggie, 'you still haven't told us what you've got to do with all this business.'

The little man shifted uncomfortably in his chair, and pushed the hat back on his head. 'Well, it's like this. You see, I'm a terrible man for dealin' in horses. I just can't resist a few quid, and I was a bit short, you know, for food and the like.'

'Don't tell me you sold them the brown pony,' said Maggie reproachfully.

'I suppose there's no use denying it. I did. I met them fellas in the town, and they wanted a good strong pony.'

'But that little pony of yours was old,' Fergal recalled. 'It wouldn't be able to hump stuff over to the Manor. Even they would know that.'

'True, true, but then I've been in this horse dealin' business a long time.'

'So you sold it to them anyway,' said Maggie, 'and bought yourself a new one.'

'Well, not exactly.' Stumpy Joe took off his hat and wiped the sweat from his brow as if he was having difficulty in finding the courage to tell them what he had done.

'What do you mean, not exactly?' asked Pernickety.

'Well, it was like this,' he said. 'I knew they wouldn't buy the pony the way it was, but I needed the money real bad. So I . . . I dressed it up a wee bit.'

'You mean that was the same pony we saw you with in town?' asked Maggie.

'The one and the same,' he said. 'You see, it had just been shod, and it was no trouble to me to do the rest. I had done it many's the time before. I gave it a good washin' and spongin' down. Then I polished its hooves and plaited its tail and mane with straw. By the time I was finished with it, the only thing it was missin' was a red rosette.'

'But, Joe,' said Maggie, 'the pony we saw was very perky. It could hardly stand still, it was so full of beans.'

Stumpy Joe lowered his head as if he was ashamed of what he was about to tell them. 'Well, to tell you the truth,' he said, 'that's an old trick. You see, all it needs is a wee bit of ginger under the tail, and it'll act like a two-year-old.'

Nadia had been listening to this strange tale in silence. Now her large dark eyes grew even larger and her mouth dropped open as she realized what the little man was saying.

A smile was creeping over the faces of the two boys, and they chuckled at the thought of it. Maggie, however, didn't find it one bit funny. 'But, Joe,' she said, 'that was a terrible thing to do.'

'Aye, I know, I know,' he admitted. 'But when you're hungry you'll do anything for a few bob. And it brought me no luck. No luck at all. When them fellas found out the pony wasn't fit for the job, they turned it loose and came lookin' for their money back.'

'So it *was* you they were chasing that day at the river,' said Pernickety. 'Not us.'

'Now you have it, Scholar.'

'Well, we told you there was a curse on the gold,' said Maggie. 'And it serves you right, after what you did to the pony.' So saying, she stuck her nose in the air and turned her head away from him.

The generator was still going, providing a fairly good light, and after a while Stumpy Joe got up and started to poke around crevices in the rocks. 'I remember,' they heard him saying, 'my grandfather telling how he picked nuggets of gold out of cracks in the rock just like these, up in the Klondike.'

The boys went over to watch as he examined various small stones and discarded them on the floor. 'Ah well,' he said, taking out a cigarette, 'some day I'll strike it rich, just like Donaghoo, and then the sky's the limit.' He struck a match, but it flickered and went out. 'My mother always warned me not to smoke,' he joked. 'She said it would stunt my growth — and look what happened.'

The boys laughed, and in spite of what he had done the girls couldn't help smiling too. He struck another match, and when it also went out he looked over at the door. Seeing that it was still closed, he whispered, 'There's a draught comin' from somewhere.'

Fergal held up his hand, and feeling a slight movement of air observed, 'It's coming from above us. Do you think there might be an opening up there?'

'Could be,' said Stumpy Joe, and as they took more notice of their rock prison they could now see that it was of a very irregular shape, with deep fissures going off here and there into the darkness.

'Here, Joe,' said Fergal. 'Give me a leg up.'

The others watched as Fergal, with Stumpy Joe's help, pulled himself up on to the rocks, and straddling them, inched his way up into the dark recesses of the cave. 'It's fresh air all right,' he told them. 'I can feel it in my face. It's getting stronger.'

Several small stones trickled down the rocks, and Maggie warned, 'Be careful, Fraggle.'

'I can see daylight,' he replied, and a few minutes later they heard him whispering, 'I'm out!'

'All right, up you go, Scholar,' said Stumpy Joe. 'And mind your glasses.' He helped Pernickety up on to the rocks, and guided him with words of encouragement until Fergal took him in hand and he went out of sight.

'Now, girl,' said the little man to Maggie. 'Do you think you can make it?'

'I can try,' she said.

Fergal now descended from the darkness and pulled Maggie up. When she had steadied herself, he worked his way around behind her and directed her strong leg on to firm footholds. Down below, Nadia and Stumpy Joe watched. 'Take it easy now, Maggie,' they heard Fergal saying. 'We're nearly there.'

A short time later, Fergal descended once more into the cave and whispered urgently, 'Now you, Nadia.'

Nadia shook her head. 'I am sorry,' she said, 'but I could not make such a climb. You go and get help.'

'Would you not try?' asked Stumpy Joe.

Nadia shook her head again. 'Forgive me, but it is too much for me.'

'It's no use,' Stumpy Joe told Fergal. 'She says she can't manage it. You go ahead. I'll stay here and make sure she's all right. Hurry now, while you can.'

Fergal turned and disappeared into the darkness again. A few minutes later, he emerged through a small opening in the rocks and joined Maggie and Pernickety on the hillside. It was bright and warm after the cave, and they shaded their eyes from the sun and took stock. There was no sign of any of the men, and Maggie whispered, 'Look, they haven't spotted the ponies yet. Come on.'

Scrambling back up over the hill, they made their way down the far side until they came to a small stream and followed it along until they reached the river. Having made sure they hadn't been spotted, they crossed the river and hurried down to where they had left the two ponies tethered to the alder tree. Maggie and Fergal mounted Silver, Pernickety took Cedar, and off they set as fast as they could for the Manor.

Paddy Mac was polishing the black limousine on the

driveway opposite the steps of the Manor when they galloped up. As they skidded to a halt, Monique appeared at the door, expecting to see Nadia.

Where's Mr. Baracat?' cried Maggie.

'I'm not sure,' said Paddy Mac. 'I think he's up at the farm, why?'

'They're holding Nadia prisoner over at the old mines,' panted Fergal.

'Quelle catastrophe!' cried Monique and ran back inside.

Startled, Paddy Mac dropped the duster and asked, 'Who is? Where?'

'Armed men,' Pernickety told him. 'Over at the old gold-mines. Tell him to ring the guards.'

'Ahmed's in trouble too,' said Maggie. 'They've hidden forged money in the plane and they're forcing him to fly it out. Hurry!'

They turned to go, and as the ponies pranced on the gravel, Paddy Mac ran over to them. Undecided what he should do, he asked, 'And where are you going?'

'To the plane,' cried Maggie. 'Hurry and raise the alarm.'

As they galloped off towards the airfield, Paddy Mac rushed into the Manor to telephone the gardai and try and locate Mr. Baracat.

Emerging from the trees, Maggie, Fergal and Pernickety could see that the plane was now parked farther out from the hanger, facing down the runway. The steps were down, but there was no sign of Ahmed, either in the cockpit or in the immediate vicinity.

'Maybe he's inside loading up,' said Fergal. 'We must tell him where Nadia is and that Paddy Mac's phoning the guards.'

Dismounting, they hurried over to the plane and climbed inside. A quick glance at the cockpit, and a look inside the cargo hold confirmed that Ahmed wasn't on board. They turned to leave and were at the top of the steps when Fergal warned, 'Here he comes! And . . . there's somebody with him. I think it's one of the gang. Quick, hide!'

Nipping into the cargo hold, they pulled across the curtain, held their breath and waited. Through a chink in the curtain, they saw Ahmed coming on board, followed by a man with a flat type of pistol in his hand. The man, who was wearing a suit, waited until Ahmed caught the hand rail, pulled the steps up into the plane and checked to see that the door was closed properly. Then he motioned with the gun for Ahmed to go to the cockpit, and following him up the aisle slipped into one of the front passenger seats where he could see everything that was going on.

Settling into the left-hand seat of the cockpit, Ahmed produced a plastic-covered booklet and began to go through a series of checks, flicking switches here and there with his right hand. From where they were, the children could see red and green lights flashing on and off, and red letters and numbers at the top of the instrument panel. Suddenly they became aware of a low whine which gradually increased in pitch, and looking out of the small oval window on their right saw the propeller starting to turn.

'He's going to take off!' whispered Pernickety.

All three had their faces squeezed against the window now. They could see the propeller gathering speed and hear the heavy-throated noise of the engine as it did so.

'What are we going to do, Fraggle?' asked Maggie.

'What can we do?' he said. 'I just hope this is the test flight Nadia was talking about, that's all.'

Peeping up the aisle, they saw Ahmed switching on the wipers to give the windscreen a quick clean. The other man was still seated. He had put away his gun and was looking out the window as Ahmed started up the second engine.

Going to the other side, the children saw the second propeller starting to turn, and a puff of blue smoke. Both engines were going now and as the second propeller gathered speed they heard Ahmed feathering the first one so that it became quieter and smoother.

Desperately they peered out the windows and looked all around in the hope of attracting someone's attention. They saw no one, and as the noise of the engines increased again, so did their panic. By now their faces had gone white, and they could not hide the fact from one another that they were almost sick with fear.

On running into the house, Paddy Mac had first telephoned the gardai and informed them of what the children had told him. Then he had rung the farm and after some delay made contact with Mr. Baracat. Mr. Baracat immediately jumped into his Range Rover and drove down to the Manor where Nadia's aunt, Paddy Mac and Monique were waiting anxiously for him on the steps. Jumping out, he asked, 'Have you phoned the police?'

'We have, sir,' said Paddy Mac. 'They're on their way to the old mines.'

They could hear the whine of the plane's engines

now, and realizing that it was getting ready to leave, Mr. Baracat got back in and shouted, 'Ring the police again and tell them it's taking off. And see if there's any news of Nadia.'

The wheels of the Range Rover sent gravel flying in all directions as Mr. Baracat jammed down the accelerator and sped off through the trees in the direction of the airfield.

By this time Ahmed had begun to taxi out into the field, and seeing that they were indeed now preparing to take off, Maggie, Fergal and Pernickety had unfolded the two seats, one on each side of the cargo hold, and were holding on for dear life.

'Look!' cried Pernickety, pointing out of the window on his side. 'It's Mr. Baracat.'

Crowding around the small oval window again, they could see the Range Rover chasing after them. Mr. Baracat was leaning out the window of the door, waving frantically to try and catch Ahmed's attention. Whether he succeeded in doing so, only Ahmed knew, but he did attract the attention of the passenger. Looking up the aisle, Maggie saw the man pull his gun, stand unsteadily at the door of the cockpit, and indicate to Ahmed to keep going.

Fergal and Pernickety, meanwhile, were waving back at Mr. Baracat in the hope of alerting him to their plight. Suddenly the sound of the engines rose to full pitch, and they raced down the runway. The Range Rover dropped back and disappeared from their view. A few moments later, they were airborne and the Wicklow hills were falling away beneath them.

Acting on Paddy Mac's first telephone call the local

gardai had notified their headquarters in Dublin. They in turn alerted the airport authorities on the north side of the city, and the Air Corps at Casement Aerodrome, Baldonnel, on the south side. They also sent armed reinforcements into the Wicklow area to secure the release of Nadia.

When the Air Corps was alerted, a Fouga jet fighter had just been rolled out on to the ramp, having been prepared for target practice at sea off Gormanston Camp in County Meath. Twin machine-guns had been mounted on the nose, and six rockets loaded into the pod beneath each wing. The pilot had taken his seat in the cockpit and was putting on his white helmet when a second message was received from the gardai stating that Mr. Baracat's plane was about to take off from the airfield in Wicklow and requesting that it be intercepted. The pilot was immediately ordered to get airborne and await instructions. Taxiing to the nearest runway, he began his take-off and was airborne in a matter of seconds. At 2,000 feet, he circled the aerodrome and waited.

Neither Ahmed nor the man with the gun was aware of any of these matters as the plane sped down the runway at the Manor and took off. They had no way of knowing that the children of the forge had escaped from the old mines, that they had raised the alarm, and at that very moment were hiding in the cargo hold.

Ahmed, however, was aware as soon as he had lift-off that he was carrying more weight than he should be, even allowing for his cargo of contraband. It puzzled him, but he was not in a position to investigate. Anyway, he was hopeful that if someone else was on board they might be able to help him.

Having taken off in a northerly direction, Ahmed had levelled out and turned eastwards. The children were looking out in the hope of catching a glimpse of Dublin airport that would tell them their nightmare was about to end. All they could see was the beautiful landscape of the Wicklow hills passing beneath them, and even as they watched they saw to their dismay that the land had suddenly come to an end and they were going out over the sea.

When the plane emerged from the hills and approached the coast, it was picked up on the radar screens at Dublin airport. The military controller there immediately informed the Air Corps that the bandit, as it was now being called, had been spotted.

As the Fouga sped off in pursuit, a series of quick calculations were made at the Air Corps. The bandit had turned south east from Wicklow Head. If it continued at its present speed it would reach British airspace in just nine minutes. However, the Fouga would take almost the same time, for even though it was going much faster it had farther to go. The Fouga would not, therefore, be able to intercept the other plane before it left Irish airspace!

10   LIKE A MILLION DOLLARS

Unaware of the drama that was being fought out to the second, or indeed that they had now become 'bandits' in the language of the military men, the children of the forge crouched in the cargo hold of Mr. Baracat's plane and wondered what their fate was going to be. All they knew was that they were being whisked farther and farther from home at an alarming rate. Then something happened which was to change their situation dramatically.

On crossing the coast, Ahmed could see bad weather ahead, and decided to climb above it. As he did so, his speed fell. This was noted on the radar screens at Dublin airport and the information was relayed to the Air Corps. Another quick calculation showed that if he maintained that speed, it would take twelve minutes before he left Irish airspace. The Fouga should now be able to overtake him!

Realizing that they were not on a test flight to Dublin airport, the three stowaways desperately pondered their predicament.

'I wonder where we're going?' said Maggie.

'Lebanon,' replied Pernickety. 'Where else?'

'But we must stop somewhere before that,' said Maggie hopefully. 'Nadia said they do the journey in stages, remember?'

'Dear knows where we'll land,' said Fergal. 'But wherever it is I'm sure the police will be waiting for us. Paddy Mac will have told the guards, and they'll have notified the police in other countries. Everybody will be looking for us.'

'I hope Nadia is all right,' said Maggie. 'I wonder if they've freed her and Stumpy Joe yet?'

'If only we could tell Ahmed that she's probably all right,' said Pernickety.

'It doesn't make any difference now,' Fergal pointed out. 'Your man's there to make sure he doesn't change his mind.'

'And we'd better sit tight,' said Maggie. 'If he sees us he's just going to have three more hostages.'

Pernickety took off his glasses and wiped a tear from his eye with the back of his hand. The others sniffed and said nothing. What could they say? They were in a terrible fix, and they could see no way out of it. They were unaware that the jet fighter was now closing in on them.

Officers at Casement Aerodrome learned that the plane had been sighted when the pilot of the Fouga radioed, 'Baldonnel Tower. This is Foxtrot 215. Visual contact with the bandit. Proceeding with the intercept.' They also knew that both aircraft were now only a matter of minutes from the point where the Fouga would have to turn back.

Suddenly Maggie spotted the Fouga drawing alongside them. 'Look, look,' she whispered, tugging Fergal's sleeve. Fergal and Pernickety squeezed their faces in beside hers and peered out of the small oval window on the left-hand side of the plane. Opposite them they could see a silvery plane with orange coloured nose and wing tips, and a large V-shaped tail. It was so close they could even see the white helmet of the pilot in the cockpit, and the numbers 215 on the fuselage just below him.

'It's a fighter plane,' said Pernickety. 'Look at the guns. And you see that coloured circle on the engine? It's the Air Corps!'

With hearts thumping, they watched the fighter plane draw slightly ahead. Wondering what was going to happen next, they went over to the curtains and peered through. The man in the passenger seat, they could see, had also spotted the fighter. He immediately drew his gun and went into the cockpit.

By now the Fouga was ahead and to the left. The pilot had been trying to call Ahmed on the radio, and having got no response, communicated with him in a language that all pilots understand. He waggled his wings to show that he was placing him under arrest, and gave a signal with his hand indicating that he should turn to the right.

Time was running out, and when there was still no response, the pilot of the Fouga reached over with his right hand and flicked a switch on the firing panel to arm the machine-guns. Returning his hand to the control column, he flicked forward the trigger that lay across the top of it and held his forefinger poised above it. He was now ready to fire.

By this time a search of the area around the hangar at the Manor had located the two ponies, but not the children, and in view of the fact that they had told Paddy Mac they were going to the plane, Mr. Baracat concluded they must have been on board when it took off.

The gardai immediately informed the Air Corps of this new development, and the word was radioed to the pilot of the Fouga, with instructions not to open fire. Glancing back at the row of small windows in the other plane, the fighter pilot spotted the faces of the children at the end one. He confirmed to Baldonnel that they were on board, returned the trigger to its slot on top of the control column, and flicked the switch on the firing panel back to safe.

While this was going on, the children were also keeping an eye on what was happening beyond the curtain. The man with the gun had motioned to Ahmed to keep going, but Ahmed had indicated with his two forefingers that the fighter plane was armed. As well as the machine-guns, both men could see that the Fouga was carrying rockets under its wings, and while they didn't know that these would not be fired, as there was no way of telling where they might land if they missed, even the man with the gun got the message. Accordingly, when the Fouga waggled its wings once more, Ahmed obeyed the pilot's hand signal and turned to the right.

In their hiding-place at the back of the plane, the children heaved a huge sigh of relief and hugged each other in a silent celebration of delight. Unknown to Ahmed and his passenger, the pilot of the Fouga was no less relieved. He had run out of time and space, and would have had to turn back anyway.

As the Fouga led the way back to Baldonnel, they recrossed the Wicklow coast east of Arklow and flew along the Vale of Avoca. While neither Maggie, Fergal nor Pernickety recognized the landscape or the fact that they weren't too far away from the forge, they were greatly comforted to see land beneath them once more.

Soon they saw the television transmitter on the mountain top at Kippure, and almost before they knew it they were going down past the green radar dome into Baldonnel. Two Land Rovers and a fire-tender had come out to meet them, and when they touched down and taxied off the runway they were escorted into the ramp.

As the engines died down and the propellers came to a standstill, the three stowaways sat tight, for they still didn't know what was going to happen. They could see soldiers armed with rifles jumping out of their vehicles and taking up firing positions behind them. At the same time the gardai arrived and ran into position beside them.

A few minutes later Ahmed, closely followed by the man with the gun, walked down the aisle and opened the door. There, to the relief of all concerned, the gunman shouted he was coming out. In the conversation that followed, the gardai ordered him to unload his gun and throw it out fast. This he did, and putting his hands in the air, walked down the steps. He was immediately arrested and taken into custody.

Hearing cries of delight from the cargo hold, Ahmed whipped aside the curtain. A broad smile broke across his face, and as he put his arms around them, he said, 'I just knew I had somebody else on board, but I couldn't imagine who it was.' He helped them out on to the steps. 'But what about Nadia?' he asked.

'She's probably safe by now,' Maggie assured him. 'Maybe the guards will know.'

At the bottom of the steps a garda officer came forward to take Ahmed into custody.

'It wasn't his fault,' Fergal told him. 'He was forced to do it.'

'That may very well be,' replied the officer, 'but you'll all have to come along to the station until we sort out who did what.'

'Have you any news of Nadia?' asked Ahmed. 'Mr. Baracat's daughter.'

'We've just had word on the car radio that she's safe,' said the officer. 'Now, what's all this about counterfeit money?'

As they looked around now, the children could see that gardai and Customs men were going up into the plane to search it.

'Nadia says it's probably in the hell-hole,' Pernickety told him.

The officer frowned. 'The hell-hole? And where might that be?'

'It's under the cargo hold,' Ahmed informed him, and a Customs officer said, 'It's all right. We know where it is.'

Getting a screwdriver from the back of his car, the Customs man went in under the tail of the plane, loosened a rectangular pattern of screws and removed a small sort of trapdoor. Nothing fell out, but when he reached up in he pulled out a number of sacks, and dropped them on the ground.

Everyone had gathered around now, including the pilot of the Fouga, and they gasped in astonishment when another Customs man opened up the sacks to reveal wads and wads of money. As someone remarked, it might be counterfeit but it looked like a million dollars.

Since the local garda station in Wicklow had become the headquarters of the investigation, that was where they had to go to have the whole matter sorted out. It was a small station, and soon it was bursting at the seams. Nadia and her father were there together with Monique and Paddy Mac; also Pernickety's parents, Maggie and Fergal's parents, their grandfather and, of course, Stumpy Joe. Everybody was hugging everybody else, and everybody seemed to be talking at the same time, asking questions and telling what they knew about what had happened. It was bedlam.

'Okay, hold it, hold it,' called the officer in charge. 'The main thing is, you're all safe. Now let's get the statements down first. Then you can all go home and talk about it to your heart's content.'

Well, it wasn't quite as simple as that, although it was a good start. When the statements had been taken, they were all told they could go, even Ahmed. However, on the way to the cars, they had to run the gauntlet of what seemed to be a seething mass of newspaper reporters and television crews who had heard the news and were waiting outside. The gardai had warned everyone not to say anything to the media in case it might prejudice any court proceedings, but the idea of speaking to a wider audience than he had ever had before greatly appealed to Stumpy Joe. Pushing back his cowboy hat, he drew himself up to his full height, which wasn't much, and gave a wonderfully colourful account of the part he had played in the episode. The reporters, of course, wanted to know more, and not knowing much more he was quite happy when an officer intervened to say that was all. Like a celebrity on the run, he jumped in beside Fergal and Maggie, and they took off after the other cars, escorted by the gardai.

Mr. Baracat's large black limousine was parked outside the forge when they arrived, and as they pulled in behind it, Paddy Mac opened the door to let Nadia and her father out.

'I really did not have an opportunity to thank you all properly,' said Mr. Baracat.

Stumpy Joe's chest was swelling with pride. He walked over, shook Mr. Baracat by the hand and told him, 'Sure it was nothin' at all. Isn't that what friends are for?'

The others were amused at Stumpy Joe's brashness, but agreed wholeheartedly with his sentiments. Excitement was still running high, and someone invited Mr. Baracat and the gardai and everyone else in for a cup of tea. Maggie could see by the way her mother was fidgeting that she had probably left the house in a bit of a mess and was somewhat embarrassed by the idea. Fortunately, her grandfather spotted the problem.

'Of course you'll all come in for a minute,' he said. 'And I'm sure you could do with something a bit stronger than tea after all this commotion.' He turned and walked in past the forge to his own house. Everyone followed and Maggie could see that her mother was greatly relieved.

The sitting-room of the blacksmith's cottage was rarely used. Everything was in its proper place, and all things considered it was a much more appropriate place for an important visitor like Mr. Baracat. He must have found the cottage very quaint in comparison with the Manor, and as he looked at the clock on the wall he must have been puzzled by the words 'mollis-corium' and 'compo' printed on it. If so, he said nothing. Instead he waited politely while the old man opened the sideboard and poured out a variety of drinks, including a drop of whiskey he kept for special occasions. 'Imagine,' he was saying to himself. 'Aeroplanes and jet-fighters. Sure I never heard the like of it.' Someone produced generous measures of orange for the children and when everyone had something to drink, he raised his glass, saying, '*Fáilte romhaibh*. You're all very welcome.'

While the uniformed gardai had remained outside with the cars, an officer from the Fraud Squad who was in plain clothes, had come in. Like everyone else, there were still a lot of questions he wanted to ask. 'I know you've given statements,' he said to the children, 'but I'm anxious to know what made you suspicious in the first place. I take it, it was the £50 note?'

Fergal nodded. 'That's right. I found it up at the Money Tree.'

'You didn't know it was a forgery until we took it into the bank,' his mother reminded him.

'I know,' said Fergal, 'but we reckoned that whoever had left it there had been making a very big wish.'

'We thought at first it was a monk we saw,' said Maggie, 'because he was sort of hooded Then we guessed who it was.'

'It was dark,' Pernickety recalled, 'but we were fairly sure from the shape of him that it was Ahmed.'

Ahmed nodded. 'Yes, it was me all right. I had the hood of my duffle coat up as I sometimes find your nights quite cold.'

The children looked at each other as if to say, so much for the Arab head-dress.

Ahmed wiped his forehead with his handkerchief, and went on, 'I was very worried. These men had approached me to do this job for them—you know, fly this counterfeit money to the Middle East. When I refused, they started to make threats.'

'What sorts of threats?' asked the officer.

'Nadia. They threatened to kidnap Nadia.'

'And they nearly succeeded too,' said Nadia.

'You mean they tried?' asked Mr. Baracat. 'When?'

Nadia lowered her head.'I am sorry, father. I should have told you. That is why I fell. I was running away from them. Maggie drove the sheep in between us, and Fergal and Pernickety helped me to get away and hide over at the Money Tree.'

Mr. Baracat shook his head as if to say he couldn't understand why she didn't tell him at the time, but put his arm around her shoulders and squeezed her arm.

'That's why they grabbed me up at the hangar,' said Maggie.

'Grabbed you!' exclaimed her mother, almost jumping off the chair. 'Do you mean to say they tried to kidnap you too?'

Maggie nodded. 'They must have thought I was

Nadia when they saw me limping over to the pony in the dark.'

'The men were in the hangar looking at the plane,' explained Pernickety. 'They must have been trying to see where they could hide the money. We thought they were the Sheik's . . er . . . Mr. Baracat's guards.'

'I have no guards,' said Mr. Baracat.

'We know that now,' said Fergal, 'but we didn't then. We thought you had them to keep people out.'

'You are all welcome at the Manor any time,' said Mr. Baracat. 'We have not closed ourselves in. It is the local people who have closed themselves out.'

'That's true,' said the old man. 'But to get back to this £50 note. How come Ahmed here left it at the Money Tree if it was a forgery?'

'They had me worried sick,' Ahmed told him. 'I didn't want to be a party to this smuggling business, and yet I didn't want anything to happen to Nadia. So I decided to make a big wish. It was for her safety more than anything else that I was wishing. However, I must have got one of their bank-notes mixed up with my own.'

'How did you come to have it in the first place?' asked the man from the Fraud Squad.

'They actually showed me some of their forgeries,' Ahmed explained, 'to let me see how good they were. I suppose they were trying to involve me, maybe even tempt me, and I managed to hold on to one of them. I thought I might be able to show someone what they were doing, but I couldn't, not with the threat to Nadia. The night I went to the Money Tree I must have taken out the first note that came to hand. It was dark and I didn't realize I was leaving the forgery.'

The officer nodded. He seemed to think it was a plausible explanation.

'Then there was all the talk about the gold-mines,' said Pernickety. 'Remember, after Stumpy Joe called in to get the pony shod? We reckoned somebody had struck it rich and that Ahmed was mixed up in it.'

'After grabbing me, they came back for Star,' said Maggie. 'We thought at first Stumpy Joe had something to do with it—sorry, Joe.'

'Ah not at all,' said Stumpy Joe. 'No need to apologize. I would have thought the same thing myself if I had been in your shoes. Anyway, you were good enough to come and warn me that you thought I might be in danger.'

Maggie smiled apologetically, and her father asked, 'So it was this gang who stole Star?'

'It was surely,' said Stumpy Joe. 'You see, ah . . .' and he looked at the children as if to say they were to leave this part of the story to him. 'You see, they wanted a good pony to take the money across country to the plane.'

'That's why they didn't bother to take the saddle,' Maggie recalled.

'Sure you wouldn't get that amount of money on a pony's back,' said the old man.

'Ah you would,' said the officer from the Fraud Squad. 'Maybe not all in one trip, but when you get into big denominations like fifties, you could fit a quarter of a million into a medium-sized suitcase.'

'Is that a fact?' said the old man. Turning to Stumpy Joe, he asked, 'And what happened your pony, the one I shod for you?'

'I sold it. Ah, but did the guards not tell you? We

saw Star grazing up near the mines when we got out.'

'Did you really?' cried Maggie. 'Is she all right?'

'As right as rain,' said Stumpy Joe, relieved that the conversation had passed on to someone else's pony.

'We'll have to go up and get her,' said Maggie. 'Silver too. She's still up at the Manor.'

'It's all right,' said her father. 'I'll look after them.'

'Maybe we could bring them back in the horsebox,' suggested Nadia.

'Good idea,' said Mr. Baracat. 'Leave it to us.'

Maggie's father thanked him, and went on, 'While we were waiting down at the garda-station for the three of you to come from Baldonnel, Stumpy Joe told us what happened when you went to the mines with Nadia.'

'Did they catch the man who was standing guard?' asked Pernickety.

The officer shook his head. 'No, they must have had a look-out somewhere. When our people arrived the place was deserted. They had a great set-up there you know. The best of equipment! But we have the printing plates, and that's the main thing.'

'They must have brought the machinery in by road,' said Mr. Baracat. 'Why couldn't they take the money out the same way, I wonder?'

'Probably didn't want to risk it,' said the officer.

'What I can't understand,' said Fergal, 'is why they should want to take forged money to the Middle East in the first place.'

'It's a good question,' said the officer, 'and I hope the gentleman we took off the plane will be able to provide us with the answer. It could be any one of a number of things.'

'Sterling and dollars are very acceptable currencies in Lebanon,' Mr. Baracat told them.

The man from the Fraud Squad nodded. 'They probably had some deal going. Some bank or property deal. Or maybe they were going to change it for gold or genuine notes. Or it could be some other currency fiddle.'

'You don't think they were going to buy arms?' asked Mr. Baracat. 'There are many of those in Lebanon, you know. Too many.'

'I doubt it,' said the officer. 'I think it would be a dangerous business trying to buy guns with counterfeit money. But you never know.'

'Have you any idea who they are?' inquired Mr. Baracat.

The officer shook his head. 'It's too soon to say. When we do we'll let you know.'

'Well, counterfeit or not,' said Fergal, 'Ahmed's wish came true. Nadia and he got out of trouble in the end.'

Mr. Baracat smiled, and helping Nadia to her feet, said, 'Perhaps another visit to the Money Tree might be in order as soon as this business is straightened out. Now Nadia, your aunt is waiting for you. Perhaps your friends would accept an invitation to come and join us in a little celebration at the Manor tomorrow so that we may thank them properly for all they have done.'

'Aye, we will surely,' said Stumpy Joe. 'It would be our pleasure.'

They all laughed and saw their visitors out to the road.

As the large black limousine moved off towards the Manor, Stumpy Joe waddled away towards town.

'Well,' smiled the old man, 'whatever about the Sheik, that's probably the last we'll ever see of him.'

The others agreed, but they were wrong! About three months later another limousine appeared in town, and peering over the steering-wheel was none other than Stumpy Joe. He was still wearing his cowboy hat, but the hungry look had gone from his eyes. He now looked like a million dollars, and so did the blonde lady beside him.

He wouldn't say what had been responsible for the change in his circumstances. There were those who were unkind enough to suggest that maybe he had got his hands on some of the counterfeit money. Some believed that perhaps he had got a reward from the Sheik for looking after Nadia up at the old mines, while others wondered if, like Donaghoo, he had come across a river that had flung forth a tribute of gold. Whichever it was, he had struck it rich, and found a very attractive companion into the bargain.

In the years that followed, the little man with the big hat continued to ramble along the banks of the rivers, just as Donaghoo had done. It was even said that he would climb the hills and watch the stars, then descend and count their numbers in the waters of the Avonmore and Avonbeg. However, unlike Donaghoo, he never disclosed the secret of his good fortune, and no one ever found out if it was stars he was counting, or nuggets of gold.

ACKNOWLEDGMENTS

During my research for this story, I was helped by a number of people, and I would like to thank them.

For information on the history of gold mining in the Woodenbridge area, Peadar McArdle, Director of the Geological Survey of Ireland, was most helpful. The Air Corps gave me every assistance when it came to working out details of the air chase, while I received valuable advice on the criminal aspects of the story from Superintendent Frank Hanlon, former head of the Garda Fraud Squad, who has since retired from the force.

The Money Tree was first shown to me by the late Tim Kelly and his wife Kathleen, of Luggacurren, County Laois, and I very much appreciate the trouble they took in doing so. A visit I paid to Kykko Monastery in Cyprus, where I saw the Healing Tree, remains a very real and fond memory, and the Abbot and my friends Dennis and Lida O'Mahony of Larnaca very kindly refreshed my recollection of the monastery and its traditions when I wrote to them.

As for the art of the blacksmith, or farrier, I am indebted to Pierie Wall of Carlow. He gave me a wonderful tour of the forge at Brown's Hilll in the course of which I got an intriguing glimpse of times past when the horse was as essential to everyday life as the motor car is today. Intriguing, too, is the rhyme of the cheapjacks, for which I must thank Billy Daly of Borrisokane, County Tipperary.

The Legend of the Corrib King

Wings that whistle, Legs that fly ...

So begins the mysterious invitation that
Cowlick and his sisters Rachel and Roisin
get from Uncle Pakie, asking them
to come to the Corrib at dapping time.
But when they get there, with Tapser and Prince,
Uncle Pakie has disappeared, leaving behind
him an even more mysterious poem ...
With their cousin Jamesie, a mine of
local information, they set out in a
horse-drawn caravan to explore the countryside
and find the missing Pakie. All they have
to guide them are the clues in the poem...

Paperback £3.95

The Legend of the Golden Key

The man is dead
  But time allows,
He'll run forever
  Beneath the boughs . . .

The running dead man is part of the Legend of the
Golden Key which, since 1798, has haunted the
imagination of successive generations.

One beautiful summer day, with swallows skimming
over the river and the willow trees in full midsummer
splendour, five young hopefuls decide to solve the
mystery of the Golden Key.

Old Daddy Armstrong tells them the story behind
the legend, a tale as old as time, of a beautiful young
girl who defies her miserly father and his promise of a
fortune in gold and chooses instead to wed her
penniless lover. The young lovers disappear, but what
of the fortune. . . .?

Tapser and his friends start their quest at the castle.
There are strange happenings in the grounds,
unexplained lights are seen from the sinister fairy fort
on Wariff Hill, mysterious sound are heard late at
night. . .

Can they solve the riddle? Will the treasure be
found . . .?

*'A delightful book . . . I can guarantee that more than the
youngsters will find it enchanting. I did . . .'* DES RUSHE,
IRISH INDEPENDENT
'A rattling good yarn, well told . . .' BOOKS IRELAND

Hardback £5.95   Paperback £3.95.

The Legend of the Phantom Highwayman

They hung him on the High Road
In chains he swung and dried.
But still they say that in the night
Some do see him ride.

In the second 'legend' adventure, Tapser visits his
cousin Cowlick in the glen, and his imagination is fired
by tales of the mysterious highwayman Hugh Rua.
Is it true that his spirit rides again?
Has the phantom any connection with the smuggling of
the 'quare' stuff from down the mountains?
'The Glen has a lot of secrets,' warns Mr. Stockman.
'And so have its people . . .'

  In *The Legend of the Phantom Highwayman,* Tom
McCaughren spins a tale of adventure set in the
beautiful glens of Antrim, that reaches its climax at the
famous Ould Lammas Fair in Ballycastle O.
Revised and enlarged edition, with new illustrations.

'Action, excitement and atmosphere in full measure . . .
magnificent cover by Terry Myler.' IRISH PRESS

Paperback
£3.95

The Silent Sea

The dairy bushes are in full bloom on Skerkin Ireland as Siobhan and Gary begin their summer holidays. There is a dramatic start as they cross from the mainland in the ferry — a black yacht is ablaze and they become interested in the fair-haired boy who is trying to put out the fire.

Uncle Bawnie and Mary Anne beguile them with stories of long ago and the legendary treasure of the O'Driscolls, but the children feel that something strange is happening on the island.

Does it involve Shelly, the marine biologist who strikes them as not looking like a scientist?
Or Pappa Doc, so knowledgeable about the movements of fish and birds, with an interest in racing pigeons?
Or their new friend, Pat Mundie?

Against a backdrop of local legend and folklore, Tom McCaughren tells a fascinating tale of suspense and action. As always, his meticulous research into flora and fauna adds a new dimension to a powerful adventure story in which the black yacht *Magic Dragon* plays a mysterious part . . .

'All the ingredients of a good adventure story. A mystery yacht, legendary treasure, pirates . . . ' SOUTHERN STAR
'Baltimore and Sherkin have gathered quite a collection of adventure stories around them over the centuries. Gary and Siobhan's modern adventure is intertwined with the old tales . . . ' IRISH TIMES

Hardback £5.95   Paperback £3.95

RAINBOWS
of the MOON

A burst of sudden wings at dawn,
Faint voices in a dreamy noon,
Evenings of mist and murmurings,
And nights with rainbows of the moon
Home – FRANCIS LEDWIDGE

Two teenagers are thrown together in violent
circumstances in a desolate and dangerous part of the
Irish border. In the dramatic events that follow,
age-old rivalries come to the surface, stirring strong
feelings and emotions and giving readers an insight into
their vastly different lives and loyalties.
The conflict between the two takes place
against the wider conflict of the 'troubles' in Northern
Ireland, as the SAS and the IRA pit their wits against
each other in a battle for a deadly secret,
a secret which, unknown to the two young people,
has come into their possession.

'The importance of this book lies in its ability to bring
both the religious and the military war home in
a non-violent way. Creates an enthralling atmosphere
in which tragedy is constantly anticipated.'

CLODAGH CORCORAN, *IRISH TIMES*

'By far the best book for teenagers on the
"troubles" that I have read.'

MARGARET PENDER, *N.I. SCHOOLS LIBRARIAN*

TOM McCAUGHREN is one of Ireland's leading
authors for young people.

He has written five adventure books for The
Children's Press – *The Legend of the Golden Key, The
Legend of the Phantom Highwayman, The Legend of the
Corrib King, The Children of the Forge, The Silent Sea.*

For Anvil Books he has written two books set against
the background of the Rebellion of 1798 – *In Search of
the Liberty Tree* and *Ride a Pale Horse* – and a highly
acclaimed thriller for teenagers, *Rainbows of the Moon;*
set on the Irish border during the recent 'troubles',
it has been translated into several languages.
His five 'fox' books (Wolfhound Press) have also
been widely translated.

His awards, apart from several short-listings, include
the Reading Association of Ireland Book Award (1987),
the Irish Book Awards Medal (1987), the White Ravens
selection of the International Youth Library in Munich
(1988), the Bisto Book of the Decade Award
(1980–1990), and the Oscar Wilde Society's Literary
Recognition Award (1992).

A journalist, Tom McCaughren is RTE's Security
Correspondent. He is married and has four daughters.